Warrior's Secret

A Dark Ages Scottish Romance

**The Pict Wars
Book Two**

Jayne Castel

Historical Romance by Jayne Castel

DARK AGES BRITAIN
The Kingdom of the East Angles series
Dark Under the Cover of Night (Book One)
Nightfall till Daybreak (Book Two)
The Deepening Night (Book Three)
The Kingdom of the East Angles: The Complete Series

The Kingdom of Mercia series
The Breaking Dawn (Book One)
Darkest before Dawn (Book Two)
Dawn of Wolves (Book Three)
The Kingdom of Mercia: The Complete Series

The Kingdom of Northumbria series
The Whispering Wind (Book One)
Wind Song (Book Two)
Lord of the North Wind (Book Three)
The Kingdom of Northumbria: The Complete Series

DARK AGES SCOTLAND

The Warrior Brothers of Skye series
Blood Feud (Book One)
Barbarian Slave (Book Two)
Battle Eagle (Book Three)
The Warrior Brothers of Skye: The Complete Series

The Pict Wars series
Warrior's Heart (Book One)
Warrior's Secret (Book Two)

Novellas
Winter's Promise

MEDIEVAL SCOTLAND

The Brides of Skye series
The Beast's Bride (Book One)
The Outlaw's Bride (Book Two)
The Rogue's Bride (Book Three)
The Brides of Skye: The Complete Series

Epic Fantasy Romance by Jayne Castel

The Light and Darkness series
Ruled by Shadows (Book One)
The Lost Swallow (Book Two)
Path of the Dark (Book Three)

Some secrets will break your heart. Friends to lovers and unrequited love set in Ancient Scotland.

Ailene is the bandrui—seer—of The Eagle tribe. With her role comes much responsibility. She lives a solitary existence and prefers it that way. Ailene doesn't realize that her best friend, Muin, is in love with her.

Muin is The Eagle chieftain's son. He's loved Ailene since they were children yet has never gotten up the courage to tell her. But with their island under siege from marauders from the mainland, he's running out of time.

It's only when Ailene dreams of Muin's death that she starts to see her best friend in a different light ... only, has her change of heart come too late?

All characters and situations in this publication are fictitious, and any resemblance to living persons is purely coincidental.

Warrior's Secret by Jayne Castel

Copyright © 2019 by Jayne Castel. All rights reserved. No part of this publication may be reproduced, stored in a retrieval system, or transmitted in any form or by any means—electronic, mechanical, recording, or otherwise—without the prior written permission of the author.

Published by Winter Mist Press.

Edited by Tim Burton

Cover photography courtesy of www.shutterstock.com

Eagle image courtesy of www.pixabay.com

Map of 'The Winged Isle' by Jayne Castel

Visit Jayne's website: www.jaynecastel.com

Follow Jayne on Twitter: @JayneCastel

***

For my Tim—who is proof that your lover can also be your best friend.

***

Contents

Maps of Scotland and The Winged Isle 13
Prologue 17
  Your Friend Forever ....

Chapter One 23
  Too Late..

Chapter Two 31
  All is not Lost..

Chapter Three 37
  Ailene Casts the Bones ....

Chapter Four 45
  An Honest Conversation ....

Chapter Five 53
  Our Old Ways ....

Chapter Six 61
  Adrift ....

Chapter Seven 69
  Through the Mist...

Chapter Eight 79
  Blood Will Soak the Earth ....

Chapter Nine 87
  Occupied Territory ....

Chapter Ten... 95
  Raising Concerns...

Chapter Eleven 103

Mutton Stew ....

Chapter Twelve 109
Stubborn ....

Chapter Thirteen 117
I Can't ....

Chapter Fourteen 123
Think Like Your Enemy ....

Chapter Fifteen 131
Turning Away ....

Chapter Sixteen 141
A Chill Premonition ....

Chapter Seventeen 151
Journeying East ....

Chapter Eighteen 157
Taking Shelter ....

Chapter Nineteen 163
Secrecy ....

Chapter Twenty 169
I Can't Breathe Without You ....

Chapter Twenty-one 175
Take Your Pleasure ....

Chapter Twenty-two 181
Let Them Come to Us ....

Chapter Twenty-three 187
Turning the Tide ....

Chapter Twenty-four 195
A Formidable Foe..

Chapter Twenty-five 203
Smoke Over Balintur..

Chapter Twenty-six 211
Defeat ....

Chapter Twenty-seven 219
Burying the Dead...

Chapter Twenty-eight 225
This is My Fight..

Chapter Twenty-nine 233
A Good Man ....

Chapter Thirty 239
Meeting with the Chieftains ....

Chapter Thirty-one 247
The Path of Vengeance ....

Epilogue 253
Curious Things ....

From the author 257
Historical and background notes 259
About the Author...263

Maps of Scotland and The Winged Isle

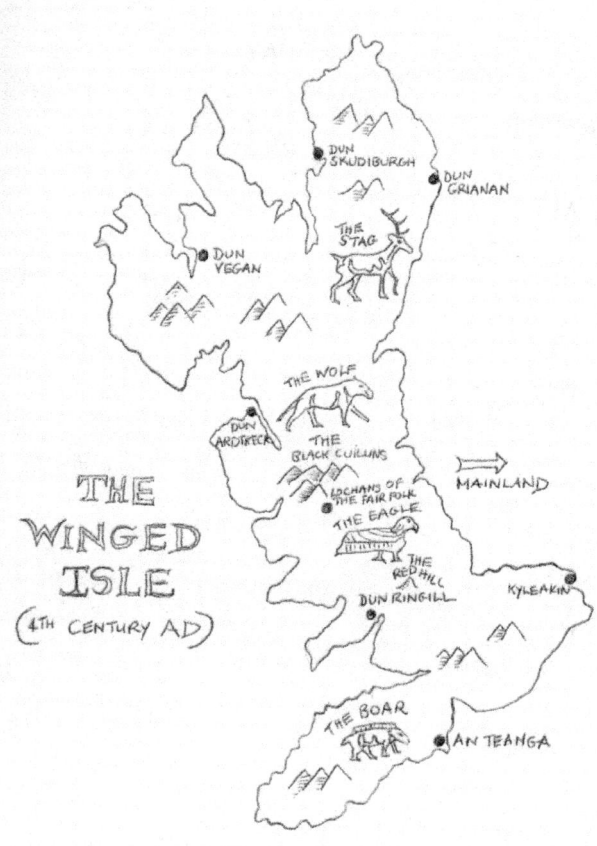

*"There are two kinds of secrets.
The ones we keep from others and
the ones we keep from ourselves."*
—Frank Warren

Prologue
Your Friend Forever

SHE'S NOT DEAD.

It did not seem real. It could not be real.

Ailene stared down at her mother's face. It looked frozen, pained. Her blue eyes stared back, glassy and unfocused.

"I'm so sorry, lass." Eithni murmured from beside Ailene. The healer placed a gentle hand on Ailene's shoulder, before she reached down and closed Mael's eyes.

When Eithni straightened up, her cheeks were wet and her chin trembled. She was one of Mael's closest friends.

Ailene drew in a trembling breath. Desperation bubbled up within her. "Stop weeping," she gasped out the words. "Ma's not dead!"

Eithni turned to her. The kindness on the healer's face, the pain and sympathy in her hazel eyes, made it feel as if someone had ripped Ailene's ribs open and grabbed hold of her heart.

It hurt to breathe.

"Lass," Eithni reached for her once more. "I'm sorry ... but she's gone. The sickness has taken her."

Ailene ripped herself free of the healer's soft touch. Body quaking, she staggered back from the pile of furs, where her mother's emaciated body lay.

"You're lying." The pain in Eithni's eyes made her want to lash out. She would not believe her mother no longer breathed. She had been around four winters when her father died suddenly, leaving her and her mother alone—it was one of her earliest memories. He had collapsed while preparing Ailene and her cousin, Talor, something to eat. When he fell, he knocked hot coals out of the hearth, setting fire to their round-house. Her mother had returned from collecting herbs to find her beloved Maphan dead and their home in flames.

Ailene had now only just turned eight. Her mother was all she had.

"Ally," Eithni whispered. "I know it's hard to accept ... but your mother's heart has stopped beating. She has left us."

"No!" The scream ripped from Ailene, hurting her throat.

Ma was not dead—only sleeping

She turned then and dove from the doorway. A grey afternoon greeted her, leaden skies presiding over frozen earth and clusters of sod-roofed huts.

"Ailene, stop!" Eithni's plea followed her, but she did not heed it. She had to flee. If she ran fast enough, maybe she could outrun the pain that dug its talons deep in her heart.

Feet flying, Ailene took off across the fort. Tears blinded her, sobs wracked her, but she did not stop.

"I knew you'd be here."

Ailene raised her head from where she had buried her face against her knees, her gaze traveling to the mouth of the cave. A lad stood there, his silhouette outlined against the darkening sky beyond.

Tightening her grip on her knees, Ailene favored the boy with a watery scowl. "Go away, Muin," she rasped.

Since taking refuge here, she had sobbed until her throat was raw and her ribs ached.

But the lad did not go. Instead, he crept close and lowered himself to the ground next to her. "Everyone's looking for you," he replied.

Ailene shifted her gaze to his face. Muin mac Galan, the chieftain's son, stared solemnly back. Five winters old, and three winters younger than Ailene, Muin had become her shadow of late—a slightly annoying one. Of course he had known where to find her; he trailed around after her like a puppy.

"Aunt Eithni is upset," he continued, slate-grey eyes observing her with a maturity that belied his years. Ailene often felt older than her eight winters; she found other girls her age annoying—and Muin was an old soul too. Instead of collecting frogs with his cousin Talor or getting up to mischief with the other lads of the fort, he had developed a fascination for Ailene. "She says it's her fault," Muin continued, "… that she didn't explain things right."

The lad spoke slowly, carefully. His face was a study in confusion. He had just reached the age where he was struggling to understand that folk did not live forever.

It was a truth that Ailene wished she was ignorant of.

"She's not to blame." Ailene bowed her forehead to her knees and closed her eyes.

"Ma says that The Reaper has taken your Ma," Muin said quietly. "Is she right?"

"Aye." The answer gusted out of Ailene. Grief sat like a boulder upon her chest. She had denied it, raged against it—but in the end she could not hide from it, even here in this cave that lay a few furlongs south of the fort. "She's gone." Her voice was weak, broken. "She's left me all alone."

A small hand, its grip surprisingly strong, fastened upon her knee. "You're not alone. You've got Ruith, and Talor, and Eithni and Donnel." He listed the names, his voice earnest. The lad paused there, his grip tightening. "And you've got me. I'll be your friend forever."

Tears leaked from Ailene's eyes, despite that she had them screwed shut. Muin, who had no idea what it was like to lose not just one but both parents, spoke those words with such conviction. As if the world was so simple.

She raised her head and looked at him. The lad stared back. A face that was so much like his father's watched her. He had Galan's long, silky dark hair too, although the determined set of his jaw most definitely came from his mother, Tea.

He looked obstinate now, almost as if he defied her to deny his words. Muin's grey eyes gleamed.

"Forever." Her mouth quirked. "That's quite a promise, Muin mac Galan."

"I mean it."

"I know you do."

His throat bobbed. "I wish I could bring your Ma back too."

Ailene's vision blurred, and she managed a wobbly smile through the tears that coursed down her face. She placed a hand over Muin's, squeezing hard. "So do I."

Sixteen years later …

Chapter One

Too Late

Late autumn, 389 AD

*Balintur
Territory of The Eagle
The Winged Isle (The Isle of Skye)*

SOME MEN KNEW exactly what to say to women. They understood the right words to make them smile, the way to approach a shy lass or to impress a cold one. Muin mac Galan reflected that he was not one such individual—although his cousin was.

He watched Talor move through the crowd, flirting with one woman before catching hold of another's hand and drawing her into the dancing.

The girl turned, her forehead furrowing at having her conversation so rudely interrupted. However, her mouth curved in delight when she saw that 'The Battle Eagle's' handsome son wanted to dance.

Muin resisted the urge to snort. *Typical.* He knew it was a bit uncharitable, but a part of him sometimes wished that one of these lasses would rebuff his cocky cousin's advances, or better yet slap his face.

But they never did.

Muin shifted his attention from the dancing and went to retrieve himself a fresh cup of mead. He was standing on the edge of the crowd, sipping the sweet, pungent drink, when Talor extricated himself from the group of eager lasses who now swirled around him and made his way across to his cousin.

"I've got a warrior's thirst," Talor announced. He helped himself to Muin's cup and took a long draft before wiping his mouth with the back of his arm. "That's better."

Muin snatched the cup back from him, before he could drain it. "Get your own drink."

Talor grinned at him. "I wish you could see your face, cousin. You look like you just stepped in a turd."

"And you're grinning like a lackwit."

Talor laughed. "Gods, you're in a sour mood tonight." He paused then, his blue eyes gleaming. "Why don't you do us all a favor and ask her to dance?"

Muin tensed, scowling. "Excuse me?"

Talor raised his eyebrows, smirking. "Every time I've looked your way tonight, you've been staring at her. I'm surprised you haven't burned a hole in her back."

Muin's scowl deepened to a glower. Times like now, he wished he had never confided in Talor. He had let it slip one night just over a year earlier after one too many horns of mead. His cousin had been sympathetic then—but he was not tonight.

"Leave it," Muin growled.

Talor's grin turned wicked. "For the love of the Gods, ask the lass to dance."

Muin stiffened, his gaze shifting to where a tall, shapely woman with sky-blue eyes and wavy dark hair chatted with Fina, another of his cousins.

Ailene, the bandruí—seer—of Dun Ringill.

The only woman he had ever loved.

Fina was recounting a tale, her hands moving expressively. The light of the Gateway bonfire that burned behind them caught the golden highlights in her hair as she talked, and gleamed off the bronzed skin of her arms. His cousin glowed like the sun, while next to her, Ailene's beauty was of a different kind—dark and mysterious, like someone had tamed the night.

Her dark hair gleamed. In daylight it was the color of peat, yet in the firelight it appeared pitch-black, making her fair skin look even paler by contrast.

As Muin watched, Ailene threw back her head and laughed, exposing a long, swanlike neck.

Muin's chest tightened. How many times had he imagined trailing kisses down that beautiful throat? He had wasted countless nights imagining what her skin would taste like.

"You'd better get in quick." Talor was back, his tone changing from teasing to warning. "Fingal is headed her way."

Muin tensed, his attention snapping to where a tall, rangy warrior swaggered through the dancers. Talor was right—he was making for Ailene.

Muin clenched his jaw. He had no claim on Ailene, to her he was nothing more than a good friend. Yet the sight of Fingal Mac Diarmid made him want to rip that man's head off.

Fingal was a warrior of The Wolf and had shadowed Ailene's step since The Ceremony of the Dead three months earlier. The ceremony had followed a hard-won victory for the united tribes against the invading Cruthini. Despite the victory, they had lost many warriors and had honored them by lighting torches around the perimeter of the camp—one for each of the fallen.

Ailene had been upset that night. Fingal had comforted her, and then later Muin had gone to check on Ailene and had seen her lead Fingal into her tent.

Muin's gaze narrowed as he stared daggers into Fingal's back. They were lovers—or had been—and the knowledge twisted like a blade in Muin's guts.

He had not known what jealousy was till that night.

"Too late," Talor said, keeping up his commentary. "You'll never get the girl if you let other men ask her to dance."

Fingal had stopped before Ailene. Head bowed, he asked her something. She looked up at him, her lovely face solemn, before nodding.

"Ally only sees me as a friend," Muin replied biting the words out with effort. "Sometimes I don't even think she realizes I'm a man."

Talor snorted, and Muin swung his gaze back to find his cousin watching him, brow furrowed. "Bitterness doesn't suit you," Talor said. "If Ailene sees you like a brother, it's up to you to change her mind."

Muin glared at him. It was easy for Talor to say that, Talor who could charm any woman he wanted into the furs. Talor who changed loves with the passing of a new moon.

Muin was not like him. He had long ago given his heart away to Ailene, and yet the thought of telling her how he felt filled him with cold dread. He would rather face a horde of howling Cruthini than this one woman.

"What if she laughs in my face?" He was not sure he would ever recover from that.

Talor shot him a frustrated look. "Ailene would never do that ... she's too soft-hearted."

"What if she rejects me?"

"Then you work to win her heart."

"And if she says she could never love me?"

Talor huffed. "Then you'd know at least and you could get on with your life." He regarded Muin then with a long, hard stare. "You can't continue this way, Muin ... pining for the lass. It'll do you no good. Talk to her ... before it eats you up inside."

Muin dragged in a deep breath, looking away. The Hag curse him, Talor was right.

Yards away, Fingal and Ailene were dancing. She swung around him, her dark hair flying behind her like a cloak.

Muin's breathing hitched. She had never looked so lovely. The glowing fire behind her highlighted her tall,

shapely figure, the swell of her full brea[st]
sleeveless leather vest she wore, and th[e]
hips accentuated by the flare of her lon[g]

Fingal noticed it too. Muin saw the [lust in]
the Wolf warrior's gaze, and the sight [made his]
hackles rise.

Aye, Talor had a point. He had to act before it was too late.

"Is that cup of mead for me?"

Ailene was out of breath as she hurried toward him, her cheeks flushed from exertion.

Muin plastered a tolerant smile to his face and nodded, holding out the fresh cup he had not yet touched. Unlike Talor, Ailene had the grace to ask. "Aye ... drink up."

Ailene took the mead with a smile. "Why aren't you dancing, Muin?" she asked before winking. "There are plenty of comely lasses out there dying for you to ask them."

Muin clenched his jaw. It was an effort not to frown, yet he quelled the urge. "I don't want to dance." The words sounded surly, and he immediately regretted them. However, Ailene merely grinned, digging him in the ribs with an elbow. "Well you're missing out ... look how much fun Talor is having."

Muin did not need another reminder of Talor's success with women. His cousin was now dancing with two lasses around the fire, twirling each in turn as they laughed and squealed in delight. Talor was wearing a self-satisfied smile as he reveled in the attention.

"He's welcome to it."

Ailene made an exasperated sound in her throat before taking a gulp of mead. "Sometimes you're such an old woman, Muin," she chided, her eyes gleaming with affection. "How will you ever find a lass to wed, if you stand glowering on the sidelines?"

An old woman.

That was one of Ailene's favorite insults for him when Muin became socially awkward.

~ 27 ~

Muin's belly clenched, although he covered up his reaction with an affable shrug. He did not like that Ailene thought him unadventurous, or that she encouraged him to find a woman to marry. "I'm a terrible dancer anyway," he muttered. "I think I'll save the lasses from having their feet crushed."

In response, Ailene merely laughed.

The sound wrapped around Muin like a lover's embrace, and he watched her, wishing she saw him in a different light.

The Gateway bonfire burned long into the night. This was the eve that marked the end of the warm months and the beginning of the bitter season.

The nights had drawn in, and the air had a bite to it this evening.

Muin left the smoldering bonfire and walked back toward the north gate of Balintur. Torches burned around the perimeter, throwing long shadows against the high wooden walls.

It was good to have something to celebrate; Gateway was a reminder that despite everything his people had been through of late, life still continued.

In the past three months Balintur had become home. The Eagle stronghold, Dun Ringill, was occupied by the enemy—the invading Cruthini, who had swept across The Winged Isle like a plague over the summer.

Muin's brow furrowed as he imagined the stacked-stone broch, the high perimeter walls commanding a view of Loch Slapin. He hated the thought of The Serpent—for that was the tribe's name—defiling his home. The image of their leader, Cathal mac Calum, seated upon The Eagle chieftain's carven chair in the feasting hall, made his belly clench.

Not for much longer.

They had rallied, had rebuilt their strength over the past three moons. More warriors had joined them from distant corners of the isle. They were almost ready to take on The Serpent again.

Two girls dressed as brownies ran past Muin as he neared the gates. His frown faded at the sight of them. One of the lasses was his wee cousin Eara.

"Goodnight, Muin," she sang out, before she and her friend burst into fits of giggles. They ran off, their silly red hats and tattered tunics flapping.

Muin's mouth quirked. Many folk liked to dress up at Gateway as brownies, selkies, and wulvers—magical creatures that inhabited the isle's loneliest places. The veil between this world and the next was at its thinnest tonight. The souls of the dead were said to walk abroad.

Leaving the last of the revelry behind, Muin entered the village. Part of him wanted to make straight for the hut he shared with Talor, for he was tired. Yet his cousin's words needled him.

You can't continue this way.

Instead of veering right, as he usually did, Muin cut left.

It had to be tonight. If he did not tell Ailene what lay within his heart now, he would lose his nerve. He reached then to the bracelet he wore around his right wrist. It was made from braided leather, with small turquoise stones interwoven through it. Ailene had given it to him at Mid-Winter Fire three years earlier.

He had never taken it off since.

He would go to her hut and wait outside till she returned home. It was getting late—she would retire soon.

Muin's pulse accelerated at the thought of facing her. He had no idea what he would say, how he would put his feelings into words.

Don't think about it. He bowed his head and plowed on, making his way up a narrow dirt street between rows of large huts. Moonlight bathed the thatch and sod roofs of Balintur, making the village look as if a frost had settled.

Ailene's hut lay against the east wall—a tiny dwelling. The bandruí lived alone as she had at Dun Ringill. The role of seer was a vital one to their people, revered.

Ailene was the only person Muin knew who did not share her dwelling with kin.

He had almost reached his destination, the glow of the torches atop the eastern edge of the perimeter growing nearer, when the sound of voices up ahead made Muin slow his step.

The gentle lilt of a female voice and the low rumble of a man's.

Muin's breathing stilled, and he drew to a halt.

Ailene. She must have left earlier. But whom was she speaking to?

Muin moved forward again, cautious now, and stepped into the shadow of the nearest hut. Then he edged closer.

Two figures stood before the entrance to Ailene's hut. The glow of the torches above outlined the seer's statuesque form—and the lanky frame of the man that loomed over her.

Muin's gut clenched. *Fingal mac Diarmid.*

The pair of them stood close, so much so that they were almost touching. Fingal's voice was an intimate murmur—a lover's tone. He spoke so softly that Muin could not make out the words.

Ailene gazed up at him, listening.

Pain gripped Muin's chest, and he realized he had stopped breathing. Slowly, he exhaled, disappointment crushing his ribs. His stomach roiled, and bile stung the back of his throat.

He was too late. Talor was right, he had hesitated too long, and now another man had claimed Ailene.

The bandruí laughed then, a soft, sensual sound that was a punch to Muin's guts.

Enough. He did not need to see any more, could not bear to.

Tearing his gaze from the couple, he turned and strode away down the shadowed street.

Chapter Two

All is not Lost

"I'VE NOT FORGOTTEN that night we had together." Fingal stepped close and gazed down into Ailene's eyes. Even in the moonlight she could see hunger there. "Isn't it time we repeated it?"

Ailene drew in a slow, steadying breath. She wished the warrior would step back; he was crowding her. She also wished he would forget that they had lain together—for it was not a night she cared to ever relive.

It had been a low point for her. She'd been upset and had thought Fingal would give her solace—yet he had not.

"Fingal." She stepped back then, wishing that she was not alone with him. "I don't wish to repeat it ... I can't offer you more than friendship. I'm sorry."

Fingal's lean face hardened, his gaze narrowing. "We aren't friends, Ailene. If you won't lie with me again, we're ... nothing."

The harshness in his voice was like a slap across the face. In an instant he had gone from charming to aggressive.

"Well, I won't," she replied firmly, her anger rising. *You goose*, she chided herself. *You should have expected this.* "It looks like we're nothing."

Fingal stepped back from her, his face thunderous. Ailene was not easily cowed, yet fear did feather down her spine then. She wished Muin or Talor were with her, or Fina. She had been a fool to let Fingal get her alone.

"Fickle bitch." Fingal spat on the ground. An instant later he turned on his heel and stalked away.

Ailene watched him go, her heart thundering. To think she had worried about sparing his feelings. Fingal did not deserve such worries. The moment he realized she would no longer spread her legs for him, he had turned nasty, revealing his true character.

This is why it's best to keep to myself. Ailene folded her arms across her chest, hugging herself tight as her vision blurred. *Foolish tears.* She was not upset over losing Fingal, only that she had lain with him in the first place.

It had been her first time, and it had not been a pleasant experience. He had been over-eager, rough, and there had been no closeness afterward. He had merely rolled off her and promptly fallen asleep. But Ailene had not slept. Instead she'd stared up into the darkness, wondering why men and women spoke of coupling as if it brought great pleasure and joy.

That had not been her experience.

Ailene turned and ducked into her hut. A cluttered yet homely space greeted her. Over the last three moons this hut had become her home, although she missed her hovel at Dun Ringill. Her home there was ramshackle, but she loved her rambling garden and the clutch of fowl she looked after. Here, inside the walls of Balintur, she often felt restricted.

A lump of peat still glowed in the hearth, illuminating the interior of the hut.

With a sigh, Ailene sat down next to the fire pit. Gateway always made her melancholy. She had lost her mother at this time sixteen years earlier. There was something about the turning of the seasons that lowered her mood too—especially when the summer ended and the days grew colder and shorter.

Old Ruith had always loved this time of year and had told her that the spirits spoke clearer between Gateway and Bealtunn.

Ailene's vision blurred once more as she thought of Ruith. The bandruí, who had taken her in after her mother died, had been irrepressible. Wise, feisty, and proud, the seer had been good to her—and when Ailene had told her she wanted to become a bandruí, she had trained her.

Ruith ... how I miss you.

The past couple of years since Ruith's death had not been easy for Ailene. Living alone, she sometimes succumbed to loneliness.

Ailene rose to her feet and crossed to a shelf that held her most prized possessions. There was a bone-handled knife that had once belonged to her father, Maphan, a bronze bracelet that had been her mother's, and a small leather pouch containing her telling bones.

Picking up the pouch, Ailene tested its weight. Then she undid the drawstring and poured out the bones onto her palm. The bones bore the symbols of her people. Some were animal symbols, others sickles, arrows and moons. Ailene's fingers closed over them. They had been Ruith's gift to her, her dying wish. However, these days she dreaded casting them, dreaded what they told.

A few months earlier, before they had been forced to flee Dun Ringill, she had cast the bones—but she had not done so since. Tomorrow though, Galan—chieftain of her people, The Eagle—would expect her to make a prediction before him and the three other chieftains: Fortrenn of The Stag, Wid of The Wolf, and Varar of The Boar.

Ailene swallowed, her fingers tightening around the bones. She was not looking forward to it.

The last time she'd cast them, she had given three predictions, and all three had come to pass.

The first was that The Eagle would unite with the other tribes of The Winged Isle against the invaders—and they had.

The second was that The Eagle and The Boar would be united through marriage—and they had, for Varar and Fina were now wed.

Her third prediction was that dark times were coming for The Eagle. This one had also come true, for they had been forced to abandon Dun Ringill.

A chill of foreboding slid down Ailene's spine. Why did she have the sense that the dark times were not yet over?

Ailene poured the bones back into their pouch and deposited it on the shelf. She did not want to give her chief more bad news. But the Gods and the spirit world cared not for her own desires. She was merely a vessel through which they spoke. And tomorrow they would.

"You didn't speak to her, did you?" Talor's voice held an incredulous edge.

Muin glanced over at the door, where his cousin had just entered, ducking his head to avoid cracking his skull on the lintel.

Muin scowled before shifting his attention back to the smoldering lump of peat in the hearth before him. "Leave it, Talor," he muttered. "I'm not in the mood."

Talor let out a derisive snort and crossed to the hearth, pulling up a stool so he sat opposite. "What happened?"

His cousin's gaze bored into him, and when Muin glanced up, he saw a stubborn expression he knew well. Talor was like a dog with a bone at times; he was not going to let this be.

Muin sighed a curse and raked a hand through his hair. "I went to see her," he replied, looking away from

Talor. He did not want him to see the look in his eyes when he told him the next bit. "But Fingal was there with her."

He heard Talor suck in a breath. "Where? In her hut?"

"No ... outside it. They were talking and laughing. I knew what would happen next so I left them to it."

Silence fell in the small dwelling he shared with his cousin, broken only by the gentle crackle of the hearth. Outside, the Gateway celebrations had died off. Most folk would be in their furs by now.

And so is Ailene ... with Fingal.

The thought made a sharp pain knife through Muin's chest.

After a long silence, Talor spoke. "I told you not to wait so long."

Muin cut him a dark look. "She probably would have rejected me anyway," he replied, his tone sharpening.

"Well, you'll never know now, will you?"

"She sees me only as a friend."

"And now she always will."

"Enough!" Muin snarled, turning on his cousin. "You've made your point."

"I don't understand you," Talor replied, exasperated. "In battle, you're a force to be reckoned with—and yet when it comes to Ailene, you let fear rule you."

Muin's expression turned baleful, yet his cousin didn't seem to notice. Instead, Talor leaned forward, resting on his thighs, gaze bright. "You can't give up at the first hurdle."

"This isn't a hurdle, you dolt. Fingal mac Diarmid is Ailene's lover."

"Is he?" Talor challenged. "I've hardly seen them together since we arrived at Balintur. Ailene doesn't have the look of a woman in love."

"And you'd know such a look would you?"

Talor answered with a smirk. "I do, actually." He paused before continuing. "All is not lost. Don't give up until Ailene tells you to your face she doesn't want you."

~ 35 ~

Muin breathed a curse and glanced away. His gut tightened as he realized Talor was right. He could not give up yet. "Sometimes I think you want to see me with my nose ground into the dirt," he grumbled. "You'll not rest until I'm a broken man."

Talor huffed, although when he answered his voice was somber. "No ... I'll not rest until I see you tell Ailene what's in your heart."

Chapter Three
Ailene Casts the Bones

AILENE HURRIED ACROSS Balintur, head bowed against the driving rain. Her feet splashed through puddles, and stinging needles peppered the exposed skin of her face and hands.

She pulled her plaid shawl close and wished she had donned something heavier before venturing outdoors. The bad weather had rolled in just before dawn, bringing with it a blast of cold air; a helmet of grey now covered the hills around the village.

Despite the foul weather, men and women still moved about Balintur. There was always something to be done here, and a swelling population of folk to house and feed. Under the shelter of a lean-to, a group of women milking goats caught Ailene's eye. The animals stood placidly while the women filled large iron pails with frothy milk, much of which would go into making fresh curd and cheeses. The hiss of the rain drowned out the rise and fall of the women's voices and the odd goat bleat.

The meeting house lay against Balintur's southern perimeter. A large round structure of stacked-stone with a conical sod roof, it was a recent construction. The four chieftains who currently resided here needed a place to meet in the village, a place where all four were on equal footing. Balintur stood on Eagle land, but Galan mac Muin shared rule here.

Splashing through a particularly large puddle, Ailene winced. Her new fur-lined boots were soaked through, as was the hem of her skirt.

She ducked into the meeting house, pushing a curtain of sodden hair out of her eyes, and ran straight into a man's broad chest.

Ailene's breath gushed out of her, and she stumbled back. She would have fallen if strong hands had not grasped her upper arms and pulled her upright.

Her gaze shot up, and she stared into a familiar pair of iron-grey eyes. "Muin," she gasped. "I'm late."

"I know," he replied, a crease forming between his dark eyebrows, "I was coming to find you."

It was then that Ailene realized she was the last person to enter the meeting house. Everyone else was seated upon stools around the central hearth—they were all watching her.

Ailene swallowed. "Apologies," she greeted them. "I overslept." She glanced back at Muin to see that his frown had deepened. He looked almost disapproving. "Well, last night *was* Gateway," she muttered.

She was surprised the four chiefs and those seated with them were so fresh-faced. Fina, seated at Varar's side, looked radiant—her golden skin burnished by the glow of the fire before her.

They were all here: Galan—his wife, Tea—and two sons Muin and Aaron sat to her right; followed by Wid mac Manus—his wife, Alana—and their only surviving son, Calum. They lost their youngest in the Battle at Bodach's Throat.

Tadhg mac Fortrenn sat directly opposite, flanked by his wife, Erea, on one side, and his two daughters on the other. Ailene noted that Tadhg was not wearing his stag's head mantle this morning, a decoration that made the man even more intimidating than usual.

The last of the four chieftains seated before the fire was Varar mac Urcal. Tall, dark, and brooding, a small silver hoop earring glittering from his left earlobe, The Boar chieftain was a man Ailene was wary of. Varar exuded raw sensuality and had an arrogance that often rubbed the other chieftains up the wrong way. However, Ailene's friend Fina had fallen deeply in love with him, and they were now wed.

Seeing them seated together shoulder to shoulder, Ailene found it hard to believe they had ever been enemies. She envied their love, their happiness. After her recent experiences, she couldn't imagine finding such joy for herself.

Varar's sister, Morag, usually attended these councils, but she had just given birth to a baby boy two days earlier—it had been a difficult birth, and Morag was still confined to her furs.

"Come forward, Ailene," Galan greeted her with a smile. "We've just started."

Ailene peeled off her wet shawl and hung it up by the door. Then she approached the fireside.

Meanwhile, Muin took his seat in between his father and brother, Aaron.

"So, as I was saying," Galan said, shifting position on his stool. "Before we make any plans, we need to be clear on what we want the next year to bring."

"That's easy," Varar mac Urcal replied, his voice edged with aggression. "Every Serpent warrior on this isle must die."

Galan cast the younger chieftain a quelling look. "Really? Could we not just drive them out, send them back across the water?"

"And give them a chance to strike back?" Wid asked, his face stone-hewn. "I agree with Varar. They invaded, brought war and death to this isle. They need to pay." The loss of a son had aged Wid. His dark mane had streaks of white through it, and his face bore lines of care that had not been there before the intruders arrived.

Silence fell in the meeting house, while the four chieftains exchanged wary glances. They were no longer at war with each other these days, although the good relations were still new and these councils were often tense.

"Well then," Tadhg said, shattering the tension. "If the goal is to wipe these invaders off our isle … the next question is when do we attack Dun Ringill?"

"It should be before Mid-Winter Fire," Galan replied.

"Are we ready?" Muin spoke up. Surprise filtered through Ailene as she watched Muin meet his father's eye. He rarely spoke up in meetings, preferring to let Galan take the lead.

The Eagle chieftain frowned, his dark brows knitting together. "Almost."

"But the Long Night's just over a moon's cycle away now," Muin pointed out.

"Aye … but if we attack any later, we'll be doing so in the snow," Wid spoke up. "Not ideal fighting conditions." The Wolf chieftain nodded to Galan. "I agree … let's hit Dun Ringill before the weather worsens."

Tadhg cleared his throat then. "Before any plans can be made, any decisions taken, a seer should read the bones. Let's see what the bandruí has to say."

It went quiet inside the meeting house; everyone had shifted their attention to Ailene, their gazes expectant.

Drawing in a deep breath, Ailene withdrew the telling bones from the pouch at her waist. A space had been cleared for her before the hearth, and she knelt there.

Ailene poured the bones into her palm. They rattled like chattering teeth, a sound that usually reassured her.

This morning, however, it just made her nervous.

Muin had looked at her before as if she had slept in out of laziness and lack of care. But the truth was she had barely slept all night. Her confrontation with Fingal had put her on edge, and then worries about this council had caused her mind to race. Eventually, she had fallen into a deep, dreamless slumber near dawn, and had awoken to find herself late.

Ailene closed her eyes and cast the 'telling bones', scattering them across the dirt floor before her.

~ 40 ~

The silence around her deepened, as it always did when she cast the bones.

Ailene exhaled slowly and opened her eyes, her gaze traveling to the floor.

For long moments she studied the bones, a chill sliding down her spine as she did so.

Gods ... not again.

"Ailene," Galan spoke up, his voice edged with concern. "You've gone pale, lass. What is it?"

Ailene sat back on her heels and placed her palms flat on her thighs. This was exactly what she had been dreading.

Swallowing, she met Galan's gaze. "I have both good news and ill news." she said. "Which would you like to hear first?"

"The good news," Wid spoke up. "If you've got something unpalatable to share, it might make it easier."

Ailene nodded. "Very well." She gestured to two bones that had fallen close to her, overlapping each other. "The mark of The Boar and that of the rising sun." Her gaze shifted to Varar mac Urcal. "This is an auspicious sign for your people."

Varar's dark-blue gaze held hers, and he inclined his head before nodding.

"And what of this ill news?" Tadhg mac Fortrenn spoke up. Like many others here his gaze was wary as it settled upon her. "Don't keep us in suspense."

I make them uncomfortable, Ailene realized. *They both respect and fear me.*

She glanced right at Muin. He was watching her steadily. Ailene dropped her gaze then, shifting it to the center of the scattering of bones. "The mark of the Eagle," she said finally, "has fallen next to the sickle and The Hag."

A breathless hush followed her words. And then Aaron, The Eagle chieftain's youngest, muttered a curse.

Galan cast Aaron a censorious look before leaning forward. His features tensed, making him look even more hawkish than usual. "So, it's as before," he mumbled. "More dark times ahead for The Eagle."

Ailene held his gaze. "Aye."

Galan sat back and raked a hand through his long hair. Then he loosed a long breath. "I'm beginning to dread these sessions, lass."

Ailene drew in a sharp breath, her chin lifting. "I might be wrong."

"You haven't been so far," Varar spoke up. "From what Fina tells me, you have been uncannily accurate."

"She has," Galan confirmed. He exchanged a look with his wife, Tea. "I suppose we should rethink our plans to take back Dun Ringill before Mid-Winter Fire then?"

Tea's proud face tensed, her full mouth thinning. "Aye ... with such a foretelling we should be wary."

"Should we concentrate on An Teanga instead?" Wid asked, scratching his bearded jaw. "The signs are good for The Boar. It seems the right time to take back their stronghold?"

A long pause followed. Those around the hearth exchanged looks, some wary, others hopeful.

"It makes sense," Tadhg spoke next. "The bulk of The Serpent's strength now lies at Dun Ringill, but if we take back An Teanga, they will be isolated, surrounded.

All gazes swiveled to Varar. Ailene noted that The Boar chief had wisely said little till now, waiting while the others talked the idea through.

"If Galan agrees, then so do I," he said after a pause. His gaze met Galan's across the hearth. The Eagle chieftain stared back. Unlike moons earlier, when the two men had been enemies, there was no animosity now.

"Taking back An Teanga seems the wisest course of action," Galan admitted. "I'll not plan an assault on Dun Ringill until the spring." He cut Ailene a glance. "Depending on what the bones tell us."

"The Boar will be at your side, whenever you decide to take back your fort," Varar answered. He shared a look with Fina before continuing. "Our people are united now. Our fates are entwined."

Galan nodded, a smile softening his hawkish features. "In the meantime, we will strengthen Balintur's defenses. If The Serpent launch an attack on us here, we must be ready."

"How will you take An Teanga back?" Wid asked Varar, his brow furrowing. "We don't know how many defend the fort, or how."

"I think it's wise to send out a scouting party first," Varar replied. "I'll take a small group south by boat. When we return, we'll plan a campaign."

"I'm coming with you," Fina spoke up before raising a hand to silence her husband's protest. "Don't bother to argue."

"As will I," Muin added. "And Talor will expect to be included as well."

Ailene suppressed a wry smile. As he was not a chieftain's son, Galan's nephew was not here to raise his hand. However, she knew he would be furious not to be included in the scouting mission.

Varar met Muin's eye across the room, before his mouth lifted at the corners. "It'll be good to have you and Talor with us," he replied.

Across from The Boar chieftain, Galan spoke up once more. "When will you depart?"

"Tomorrow at dawn," Varar answered. "The sooner we find out how heavily defended An Teanga is … the sooner the fight to retake this isle can begin."

Chapter Four

An Honest Conversation

"AILENE ... WAIT!"

HALTING her step, Ailene cast a glance over her shoulder. That meeting had drained her; she just wanted to be alone in the aftermath. Not only that, but the rain was coming down harder than ever.

She was now utterly drenched.

A tall, broad figure approached. Clad in a leather vest, plaid breeches, and fur cross-gartered boots, Muin was soaked. The rain ran down his face and shoulders and had plastered his long dark hair against his scalp.

"Muin," Ailene greeted him with a sigh. "What is it?"

He wore a serious expression; his slate-grey gaze shuttered. "I need to speak to you."

Ailene suppressed a sigh. As fond as she was of her friend, the last thing she needed was a discussion about what she had foretold. She could not tell him any more than she had told the others. "Now?"

"Aye."

Ailene blinked away the rain that was now running into her eyes and pulled her sodden shawl around her—

not that it did much good against such a torrential downpour. "Come on then," she muttered. "My hut is the nearest."

Muin ducked his head and followed Ailene into her hut. The smell of dried herbs enveloped him, and he inhaled deeply. The scents of vervain, mint, and primrose—all sacred herbs she used in her role as seer—would always be ones he associated with Ailene.

Pulling the door closed behind him, he straightened up. He then realized he was dripping water all over the floor.

"Here." Ailene favored him with a rueful look as she passed him a drying cloth. "You could do with this."

"Aye." Muin cast her a grateful smile. Their knuckles brushed as he took the cloth. Muin's breathing caught, but Ailene was already turning away, retrieving a cloth for herself.

Muin dried his face and arms. But as he toweled off his long hair, his gaze kept returning to Ailene.

She had peeled off that wet shawl and hung it up to dry. Now she stripped off her leather vest, and Muin went still.

Underneath, she wore a sleeveless linen tunic.

It was wet and had plastered to her breasts.

She may as well have been standing before him naked from the waist up. As she turned, reaching for a dry woolen shawl hanging from the wall, Muin saw the swell of her high, full breasts, her pink nipples visible through the transparent fabric. Muin's reaction to the sight was instant and unbidden. His breathing caught—and his shaft turned rock hard.

Ailene turned away from him, walked over to the corner of the hut, next to the pile of furs where she slept, and stripped off the tunic.

Heart hammering, Muin glanced down at the rigid bulge in his breeches. The material was sodden and left little to the imagination as it was.

As soon as Ailene turned round, she would see it.

The Reaper take me.

Muin had come here to speak plainly to Ailene, to show her what was in his heart—not what lay in his breeches.

He had to do something about this, or he would never be able to look her in the eye again.

When Ailene turned around, she found Muin seated on a stool by the fire, leaning forward and drying his hair vigorously.

Ailene had draped a woolen shawl around her shoulders and pulled it closed over her naked breasts. However, their lush curve was still visible. The shawl just had to slip an inch or two and one of those rosy nipples would peek out.

Muin swallowed hard. This was torture.

"You have beautiful hair," she said with a smile, taking a seat opposite him. "Long and silky ... just like your father's."

Muin answered with a strained smile. She talked to him as if he were her brother. The fondness on her face made a splinter of despair lodge itself in his heart. He wanted to see her pupils dilate at the sight of him. He wanted her to reach out and touch his hair with a sigh of need. He wanted her to tangle her fingers in it as he took her on the floor of this hut.

The ache in Muin's groin brought him up short. He needed to stop these thoughts, or he would not be able to move from this stool.

"Shall I warm us some mead?" Ailene asked.

He nodded, grateful for the distraction. "Aye, thanks."

His gaze tracked her as she retrieved two cups, poured some mead into an iron pot, and hung it over the glowing lump of peat in the hearth. She had to constantly adjust her shawl so it kept her covered. However, she didn't seem anxious about the fact that she might accidentally reveal her breasts to Muin.

Muin's throat constricted. Ailene was so comfortable around him, he wondered if she could ever see him as more than a friend.

"What did you want to speak to me about?" Ailene sat down once more and placed the empty cups by the hearth, waiting to be filled once the mead had warmed. "Is it about my predictions?"

He shook his head. Since entering the hut his throat had closed up. He had barely spoken two words. However, his gesture made relief suffuse Ailene's face. "Thank the Gods ... I'm worn out. I don't think I could stand to talk about it again today."

He forced a smile, although inside his guts were tying themselves in knots. "Then we'll talk about other things."

She watched him expectantly, her blue eyes guileless and trusting.

Muin knew he was about to ruin their friendship, but he could not keep it inside him any longer. "Ally," Her name came out like a croak so he tried again. "Ally... I'm in love with you."

Silence fell in the hut, and for a long moment she merely stared at him.

Muin suddenly became acutely aware of the rasp of his breathing, the thunder of his heart, and the lashing of the rain against the walls of the hut.

But Ailene remained silent.

Muin swallowed once more, forcing himself to keep his gaze steady. He would not be afraid of his feelings or shy from them. She would know the truth. "I've loved you for years," he plowed on, "but always from afar. Once I thought that was all I needed, but these days I must face the truth. I need you like air. Being around you and not telling you is killing me."

Her lips parted in wordless shock, and her gaze widened. Yet, still, she did not speak. Instead, her gaze roamed over him as if she was seeing him for the first time.

But the silence was damning, and Muin knew in his bones what it meant.

Ailene's gaze guttered, a shadow moving over her sea-blue eyes.

"Oh," she said softly. That one word was like a knife to the guts. He could not bear to hear any more, yet he could not move. He could only sit there and watch her crush his dreams. "I never suspected ... not even for a moment," she whispered. "How could I be so blind?"

His mouth twisted. "I hid my feelings well ... Talor tells me so."

She sucked in a breath at the mention of their cousin. Ailene and Talor's mothers had been sisters, whereas Talor and Muin's fathers were brothers. "Talor knows about this?"

Muin nodded.

Ailene rocked back on her chair and ran a hand over her face. "That's a heavy burden to carry. Why didn't you tell me before?"

"I thought I could master it," he replied. "And I tried ... but I can't."

She favored him with a pained look—a look that held no yearning for him, only a veiled pity.

Muin's hands gripped the drying cloth he was still holding.

He did not want Ailene's pity.

"You can't love me in that way, can you?" It split him in two to ask the question, but he forced himself to.

She shook her head, eyes glittering with tears. More pity. He could not stand it.

Muin leaned forward, his gaze snaring hers. "Why? I'm not your brother or your cousin. Why couldn't you see me as a lover?"

Her face went rigid at the question. "I've known you too long," she whispered. "I just can't."

Muin had heard enough. He suddenly felt brittle, as if one more word from her would shatter him into pieces.

But then, as Ailene continued to stare at him, the shawl about her shoulders slipped, revealing a creamy, pink-tipped breast. Muin sucked in a deep breath as his groin started to throb once more. Ailene was watching him so intently, she hadn't even realized what had happened.

Muin focused on her face. "I'll leave you now," he rasped, and stood up.

The moment he rose to his feet, Muin regretted his action.

He was so upset, he had forgotten his arousal. It had not subsided. And Ailene's gaze was level with it.

Her eyes widened, her lips parting in wordless shock.

A chill washed over Muin, and he looked down.

His erection thrust out against the wet plaid of his breeches—impossible to ignore or deny.

A wave of sickly heat crashed over Muin, dousing the chill.

He would have thought her rejection would have calmed his body's physical reaction to Ailene, yet it had not. His body did not care she did not want him, did not see him as a lover.

His fears had been realized: Ailene didn't see him as a man.

Although she was in no doubt about his sex right now.

A weighty silence fell.

Muin was momentarily frozen in place. He would not apologize, would not cringe or cover himself up—that would only make this worse. It would make his humiliation complete.

Yet he flinched on the inside.

Right now, all he wanted to do was find a high cliff and hurl himself off it.

This changed everything between them.

Without another word, Muin stepped away from the hearth, walked to the door, and let himself out into the drumming rain.

Ailene did not move, long after Muin had left her hut. She was stunned first by his admission, and then by—
Gods ... it was huge.

Shakily, Ailene reached for the pot of warming mead and froze. Glancing down, she saw that her shawl had slipped. Her right breast thrust out; her nipple pebbled in the damp cool air.

Heat flushed across her chest, and she yanked her shawl closed. *Was that what caused it?*

Ailene filled a cup to the brim with mead and drank deep.

She closed her eyes and then snapped them open again. That was no good. The moment she closed her eyes she saw it—that bulge in his breeches.

For her.

Ailene choked out a curse, drained the cup, and poured herself another.

This day had not started well, but it had just gotten so much worse.

Muin, her oldest and dearest friend, was in love with her. He lusted after her.

Ailene's cheeks burned when she remembered how she had stripped off her sodden vest and tunic upon entering the hut. She now wished she'd donned a clean tunic instead of throwing the flimsy shawl around her shoulders.

"The Hag curse me." Ailene's fingers tightened around the cup. "How could I not have seen it?"

Even Talor knew. Who else did?

They all probably thought Muin had a possibility, that her sisterly feelings toward him would go once he professed his love.

Ailene squeezed her eyes shut, her fingers clenching around her cup.

But they would not.

She did not see Muin as a lover. He was her friend, someone she could always rely on if she needed him. He had been kind to her over the years, especially in that dark time after her mother died.

The thought of him being anything more was terrifying, although the hurt she had witnessed in his eyes had cut her deep.

She did not want to be the one to break his heart, and yet she just had.

Chapter Five
Our Old Ways

TALOR TOOK A step back and crouched low, swinging his wooden practice sword in taunting circles. "Think you can take me on?"

A few feet away, Bonnie gave her half-brother a toothy grin. "I *know* I can."

"Go on, lass," Fina called out. "Wipe that smirk off his face."

Looking on, Muin watched the young woman circle around her opponent. Bonnie was young, but already a fierce opponent. Like her cousin Fina, she dressed lightly for training in a short plaid skirt and leather breast binding. Her long walnut brown hair swung around her in thin braids as she ducked forward, swinging her wooden blade under Talor's guard.

It was a chill morning. A raw wind blew in from the north, gusting over the thatched roofs of Balintur. However, despite her naked arms and legs, Bonnie paid the wind little attention. Her finely featured face, so much like her mother's, was taut, her hazel eyes fierce.

Talor countered her attack and swung around, twirling his sword as he did so.

"Show off!" Fina jeered. "It's a sword, not an axe. Those moves will get you into trouble one day."

Despite his dark mood, Muin's mouth curved. Talor loved to add a bit of spectacle to his fighting. Instead of a sword, his favorite weapon was a one-handed axe made of iron; the weapon was double-edged with jagged teeth along one side. It was particularly lethal when Talor went for his enemy's throat. And his cousin liked to fight with two of them.

Clack. Clack. Clack.

Brother and sister went at each other with savage intensity.

Watching them, Muin noted how light on her feet Bonnie was. Like Fina, she made up for her smaller, lighter build by being blindingly fast. And like her older cousin, her bare arms and legs were strong and finely muscled.

"He favors his left side," Muin called out as Talor deflected a particularly vicious blow with his shield—a rectangular shaped slab of oak, with leather stretched over its front and a gleaming iron boss.

"Traitor," Talor grunted. "Once Bonnie eats dirt, I'll deal with you."

"Fighting words," Bonnie snarled. A heartbeat later her wooden blade smacked into Talor's ribs. She'd taken Muin's advice, and had also used her brother's momentary distraction to her advantage.

Talor hissed a curse, his own blade swiping around to return the blow. However, Bonnie had shifted in close, under his guard. She drove a sharp elbow into her brother's belly and barreled into him.

The pair toppled onto the muddy ground.

Fina whooped and applauded from where she stood, leaning up against the stacked-stone wall of the armory. "Where did you learn that move?" she cackled, her grey eyes alight.

"Muin," Bonnie announced, rolling off Talor and climbing to her feet. She grinned across at Muin then, awaiting comment.

Despite that he had awoken with a headache, and that the world seemed a heavy, oppressive place this morning, Muin favored her with a tight smile. They had practiced that move countless times during practice sessions of late. He was impressed that she had managed it so smoothly, especially against Talor.

"Well done," he said.

"That wasn't a fair fight," Talor complained. He sat up, wincing as he rubbed his ribs.

"My favorite kind of combat," Fina quipped. "That's why you never want to face a woman to the death ... we always fight dirty."

Talor muttered a curse under his breath and rolled to his feet. He was now covered in sticky black mud. The rain from the day before had turned the streets of Balintur into a bog. Around them, the clang and rasp of iron blades being sharpened rose into the cool morning air; a reminder that the shadow of war loomed over the village.

"What did you say?" Bonnie shrugged out her shoulders and adopted a fighting stance once more, shield and blade at the ready. "Want to go again?"

Talor's handsome face screwed up, and he was about to reply when a loud noise cut him off.

The wail of a horn echoed across Balintur. It was a long, drawn-out, haunting sound that made the hair on the back of Muin's arms prickle.

Varar's scouting party was to depart.

Fina pushed herself up off the armory wall, her face suddenly serious. "I'll spar with you when we get back," she promised Bonnie with a wink as she skirted the edge of the enclosure. "Let's see if I can teach you a few more dirty tricks."

Talor groaned at this.

Fina ignored him and strode away from the training yard.

Muin fell into step with her, with Talor just a few steps behind. Walking shoulder-to-shoulder, they headed toward the gates of Balintur, where Varar would be waiting. On the way, they passed a wide lean-to where men and women were fastening iron tips to ash spears, stringing bows, and fletching arrows. The preparations for battle were always endless. Waving to the warriors, Fina and Muin walked on. As they navigated a network of narrow, muddy lanes flanked by squat stone huts, Fina cast Muin a speculative look.

"Something's amiss with you today," she observed. "You usually love seeing Talor bested, but you barely raised a smile."

"I'm fine," he grunted.

"Aye, and if that groove between your brows gets any deeper, it'll be permanent."

Muin scowled, inwardly cursing Fina her perceptiveness. Like Talor she knew him too well. Even if he tried to hide his bleak mood, she sensed it nonetheless. Muin shrugged. "I'm just preoccupied ... that's all. Ailene's reading of the bones yesterday concerned me."

Fina frowned. "Aye ... I hope she's wrong about there being dark times ahead ... but until now her tellings have been accurate."

"So you think taking An Teanga back first is the right choice?"

His cousin nodded. "With The Boar broch secured, all the tribes of this isle are stronger. Whatever happens, Varar will stand with us." She paused there, pride flickering in the depths of her grey eyes. That eye color—storm-grey—was distinctive in his family, passed down through the chieftain's line. All the Mac Muin brothers had those eyes, as did Muin himself. He was named after his grandfather, who had died a couple of years before his birth.

"Us?" Muin's mouth quirked. "You keep forgetting ... you're one of The Boar now."

Fina raised an eyebrow. "I'll always be an Eagle, cousin." She patted the mark that had been inked upon her right bicep. "Just like you."

Muin smiled. He too bore the mark of The Eagle, although unlike most warriors, who wore it on their bicep, he wore the tattoo across his chest: two spreading wings.

They were approaching the gates now, and up ahead Muin spied the tall, broad-shouldered silhouette of Varar mac Urcal.

"Muin!"

The sound of a woman's voice made Muin's spine stiffen—it was familiar, one that he knew as well as his own.

Reluctantly, he slowed his pace and let Fina go on ahead. Meanwhile, Talor stalked by, casting Muin a sly smile as he did so.

Thank the Gods that he'd had the wisdom not to confide in Talor about yesterday's disaster. His cousin didn't know that he had finally dredged up the courage to face Ailene, and nor did he know about what had happened once he did.

It was a secret that Muin hoped he would take with him to his cairn.

Ailene was the last person he wanted to see right now, and yet there she was walking toward him.

The Reaper strike him down, but his breathing still quickened at the sight of her. He tracked her progress toward him.

Comely in an ankle-length tunic made from blue plaid, Ailene held up her skirt as she walked to prevent the hem from dragging in the mud. She wore fur-lined boots, and a fur stole around her shoulders. A wide leather belt cinched in the waist of her tunic, accentuating her curves.

Ailene's peat-brown hair was loose, and it fell in heavy waves around her shoulders.

However, her finely featured face was tense this morning, her gaze clouded. She wore a determined expression that made nervousness curl up from the pit of Muin's belly.

"Are you off then?" she asked, slightly breathless. He wondered if she had hurried here to intercept him when she had heard the horn.

Muin nodded. The less said the better. After yesterday's disaster, he could barely meet this woman's eye. However, he forced himself to do so. He had laid out his soul to her, and then given her unintended physical proof of his desire for her. The humiliation still stung, yet he wouldn't stand there staring at his boots.

He would not let her see how she'd wounded him.

"How long will you be away?"

"A few days," he replied, deliberately keeping his voice aloof. "We need to scout out their defenses and discover just how big the garrison at An Teanga is before we return."

Ailene observed him. He could see concern in her lovely blue eyes; their shade always reminded him of a summer's sky. "I just wanted ..." she began awkwardly. "I wanted to apologize for yesterday."

Muin swallowed. His body tensed. The Reaper's cods, why was she bringing this up? "No need," he grunted, taking a step back from her. "Look, Ailene ... I've got to go."

Her eyes widened, and she moved forward, following him. "I know, but I don't want this to change things between us ... for it to ruin our friendship."

Muin quelled the urge to bark a laugh. "Of course it changes things."

Ailene's expression clouded, her eyes narrowing. "Why?" she demanded, a challenge in her voice. "We've been friends our whole lives. I know you're hurt now, but ... with time ... we can go back to our old ways."

Muin stared back at her, clenching his fists by his sides. This conversation was getting harder by the moment. It hurt to breathe; he felt as if he had a boulder on his chest.

Ailene's features tightened when he did not reply. "I'm sorry I hurt you," she said stiffly. "You just took me by surprise ... that's all. I was blunter than I intended."

"Muin." Varar's voice boomed across the street toward them. "Are you coming?"

Never had Muin been so grateful to be interrupted. "I've got to go," he muttered.

"See you in a few days then?" Ailene asked.

Muin gave a curt nod. He then turned and strode over to where the rest of the scouting party—Varar, Fina, and Talor—stood waiting by the gates.

The entire way there, he felt Ailene's gaze boring into his back.

Chapter Six

Adrift

AILENE WATCHED MUIN walk away and fought down irritation. However, underneath it all, hurt simmered.

The stiff set of Muin's shoulders told her that he hadn't welcomed the conversation. She had seen the horror in his eyes as she had approached. He looked as if he wished to flee from her.

The group at the gates spoke together for a few moments. Varar had chosen a small party for this scouting mission; a wise choice, for the Cruthini would have An Teanga well-guarded. It would be difficult to slip in and out unseen, and to get close enough to the broch to get a clear idea of their defenses.

The Boar chieftain was speaking to his three companions, his expression intent. Fina, Talor, and Muin listened wordlessly.

Bring them back safe.

She barely knew Varar and was still wary of him in many ways, yet the thought of Fina, Talor, and Muin never returning from this mission made her chest constrict.

Irritated at herself for worrying about such things, Ailene twisted on her heel and marched back the way she had come.

She had woken up feeling on-edge, a nagging sense of dread pulling at her belly. Yesterday's council, and then Muin's revelation, had completely thrown her. She felt as if something was wrong, and yet couldn't say exactly what.

I wish you were here, Ruith, she thought, her lips pressing together. *I sometimes feel out of my depth.*

In all the years Ruith had been bandruí of The Eagle tribe, Ailene had never seen her falter or doubt herself. But then, the tribes had never faced anything like this before.

Brow furrowed, Ailene made her way through Balintur's muddy streets. The shouts of warriors as they sparred in the training yard echoed over the village.

Ailene was halfway back to her hut when a group of children barreled toward her. She recognized Eara, Eithni and Donnel's youngest daughter, among them.

Tiny with long dark hair that flew behind her, the lass squealed as she slipped and slithered in the tacky mud.

She was the smallest of the group of bairns and was having trouble keeping up with them. The scrunched-up determination on her face made Ailene's brow smooth.

Eara was a delight.

Already she was showing an interest in her mother's healing herbs and practices. Unlike her elder sister, Bonnie, who had always wanted to follow her father and become a warrior, Eara would likely apprentice at her mother's side.

At the thought of Eithni, her people's healer, Ailene felt a little of her tension ebb.

Instead of continuing back to her hut, where she would be alone with her uneasy thoughts, Ailene turned right into a narrow lane.

Donnel—The Eagle chieftain's brother—Eithni, Bonnie, and Eara lived in a large round-house at the end of it. Even though the dwelling was larger than most in the village, it was still cramped, so Talor no longer lived with them. Instead, he shared a hut with Muin.

Ducking through the open doorway, Ailene found Eithni standing at a long table in the corner of the main living space. She was pounding herbs with a wooden pestle and mortar, while behind her an iron pot bubbled over the fire pit.

Ailene sniffed, her belly rumbling. "Is that boar stew?"

Eithni glanced up and smiled. "Aye ... you're welcome to join us for the noon meal later."

Ailene found herself smiling back. "Thank you, I'd like that."

She had not had much appetite for her usual oatcakes and honey at dawn. It would be a pleasure to join Eithni and her family for a meal rather than eat yesterday's stale oatcakes and cheese when she got home.

"Take a seat," Eithni said, reaching for a pinch of something, which she added to her mortar, before continuing to pound. "I don't suppose you could poke the fire?"

Ailene did as bid, reaching for an iron poker and prodding at the lump of peat that burned there.

"You're a little pale this morning," Eithni observed, pausing in her mashing a moment. Her delicately-featured face tensed, her warm hazel eyes narrowing. "Are you feeling unwell?"

Ailene huffed. "I'm well enough."

She should have known Eithni would note that something was amiss. As a healer, the older woman was finely attuned to the emotional and physical states of those around her.

Eithni put down her pestle, wiped her hands on a cloth, and moved across to the fire. She then settled herself down on a stool opposite and fixed Ailene in a level look. "Tea told me about yesterday's meeting," she said, her gaze shadowing. "I wish the bones had better news."

Ailene's lips thinned. "As do I."

"Donnel tells me it's a good thing that the chieftains have made a plan," Eithni continued, "but to be honest the thought of more battles ... more bloodshed ... just sickens me."

Ailene nodded. She could not agree more. "The peace was never going to hold," she replied with a sigh. "The chieftains won't rest until Cathal mac Calum and his horde are crushed."

"So, they'll attack An Teanga before Mid-Winter Fire?"

"Aye ... it looks like it."

Silence fell between the two women, and Eithni's brow furrowed. She focused upon Ailene then before inclining her head. "You're not just worried about the coming conflict, are you?" she mused. "There's something else?"

"No, there isn't," Ailene replied, waving her away with a nervous laugh. "Stop fussing."

She wanted to tell someone about Muin's confession, yet this was not the right moment.

"Your face betrays you." Eithni shook her head, folding her arms under her breasts. "You've got dark smudges under your eyes. Are you sleeping?"

Ailene pulled a face. "Not much ... I've got a lot on my mind."

Eithni's expression clouded. "We all do."

Ailene dropped her gaze to the glowing lump of peat. "I'm the only bandruí here ... it's a lot of responsibility to shoulder."

"The other chieftains left their seers at home for a reason," Eithni replied, her heart-shaped face growing solemn. "Too many predictions can confuse things ... they trust the bandruí of The Eagle ... and for good reason."

"But what if I accidentally steer them wrong?"

"You won't, lass. You may be young still, but you have a close bond with the spirit world. Ruith was always impressed with your skills."

Ailene ran a hand over her face. At twenty four she didn't feel so young anymore; most women of her age were already wed with a clutch of bairns pulling at their skirts.

"There have been so many changes of late," she said after a long pause. "I feel uprooted."

Eithni sighed, understanding lighting in her eyes. "Aye, I know what you mean. How I miss our home in Dun Ringill, with its rambling garden."

Ailene's mouth curved into a soft smile at the thought of her own small hut in the fort. It sat next to Eithni's much larger dwelling—Donnel had added extra rooms onto that hut over the years. She too had a garden there. The hut sat apart from the other dwellings in the fort, near the eastern walls. After her mother had died, she had gone to live there with Ruith. She hated to think of the Cruthini living there now.

"I too am a woman who resists change." Eithni smiled at her then, her eyes crinkling in the corners. "Give my sister a blade and a shield, and she'll go anywhere, live anywhere, but I've always preferred home and hearth. There's nothing wrong with it, but it does mean we often feel adrift at times like this."

Muin followed his companions across wind-seared hills. A short distance from Balintur, they reached the coast and descended a steep bank to where a single rowboat sat upon the rocks. The sea beyond was rough and grey, and seabirds screeched and wheeled overhead.

Frowning, Muin took in the choppy water and the rough surf that broke against the rocks.

"Not the best weather to be taking to the water," Talor commented, echoing Muin's own thoughts.

"I'd prefer to wait until a windless day," Varar replied, glancing back at Talor over his shoulder as he picked his way across the slippery rocks. "But this time of year, this is the best we can hope for."

"Aye," Fina replied, her gaze scanning the cloudy sky. "And from the looks of things, we shouldn't have any rain ... for today at least."

Varar reached the boat and shouldered off the heavy pack he had brought, which contained rations since they would not have time to fish or hunt for food. Then, Fina climbed in and picked up the oars.

Together, the three men heaved the wooden rowboat off the rocks and towed it into the surf. Muin waded in, inhaling sharply as the gelid water soaked through his plaid breeches and bit into his skin. The water of the sea and the lochs around The Winged Isle was cold all year round, but now on the cusp of the bitter season, it was freezing.

Beside Muin, Talor breathed a curse.

However, once they waded in there was no going back, and since Varar did not mutter a complaint, neither Muin nor Talor was about to. Despite that The Eagle and The Boar were friends these days, the old rivalry was not yet forgotten. Talor especially was highly competitive where Varar was concerned.

They pushed the boat through the foaming surf and then, when they were far enough away from the rocks, climbed on board.

Fina then turned the boat around and rowed them out into the open sea.

It was hard going. The wind seemed stronger out from land. It stung their exposed faces and slowed Fina's progress. As soon as they had moved away from the shore, Varar picked up a second pair of oars and started to row in unison with his wife.

The boat bobbed, rolled, and dipped in the choppy seas, yet slowly, they inched their way west, circuiting the peninsula that jutted out from the mainland. Once they rounded its western tip, they would then row south, making for Boar territory.

Later on, Talor and Muin would take their turns at rowing, but for now Muin merely clung on as the boat pitched and rolled. Queasiness rose within him, but he kept it at bay by making sure his gaze fixed upon land and sucking in deep lungfuls of cold, briny air.

It helped—a little.

At least the nausea took his mind off what he had left behind and his humiliation.

Part of him never wanted to return to Balintur. If they had not been so preoccupied with the invaders, he would have been tempted to take a year-long hunting trip to the isle's remote north. Anything to avoid Ailene.

Eventually, they rounded the rocky headland before rowing across the wide mouth to Loch Slapin.

Muin shifted his attention east, his gaze narrowing. Dun Ringill was there, just out of sight, perched like a great watchtower on the cliffs above the loch.

"Don't worry ... we'll get it back," Talor's voice intruded.

Muin tore his gaze from the eastern horizon to meet his cousin's eye. Talor had a look he knew well: both stubborn and fierce. There was no doubt in his expression, only determination.

"Once An Teanga is liberated, only Dun Ringill remains," Talor reminded him. "We'll surround them ... starve those dogs out if we have to. The fort will one day be ours again."

Looking away, Muin glanced east once more. Longing for his home rose up within him with such force it made his chest ache. "Aye, it will," he murmured.

Chapter Seven

Through the Mist

BALINTUR FELT EMPTY without Fina, Talor, and Muin.

After the noon meal, Ailene took a walk through the fields outside the walled village. Usually, Fina would have accompanied her, for it was the time of day when the two women often chatted together before afternoon chores began. However, today Ailene strolled alone.

Her gaze went to where men were shoring up the high wall that encircled the village. They were digging a ditch around the base of it, which they would later fill with iron spikes.

But those men were not the only people working outdoors. As Ailene cut a path through the fields, she passed folk bent over beds of cabbage and turnip. The last of the harvest had been reaped, yet there were still a few hardy vegetables that grew over the colder months. She also passed women and children carrying water up to the village from a well outside the walls.

Carrying a basket looped over one arm, Ailene made a mental note to stop and help herself to a cabbage on the way home. She would make a pottage for supper.

However, the basket was not for vegetables, but for collecting herbs. Every so often, Ailene would venture out in search of special plants, which she used in her role as bandruí.

The nearest woodland was an oak thicket a few furlongs north-east of the village. It was a decent walk, although Ailene was glad to stretch her legs.

Her stocks of herbs were starting to get low, and there were a few items that she did not want to run out of. Ruith had spent years teaching Ailene the properties of the many herbs she grew in her wild garden. But without her garden, Ailene had to go farther afield to gather the herbs she needed.

Reaching the woods, Ailene inhaled the fresh earthy scent of the copse. Around her rose a sea of spreading oaks. Most of them had nearly lost all their leaves, their majestic branches creating a canopy overhead.

The strain of the past few days eased. Oak woods were sacred places for bandruí. They considered oaks the king of all the trees. Often, if Ailene felt confused and in need of clarity, she would visit the nearest oak tree and sit down under it. The calming shade of a mighty oak made decision-making much easier.

Ailene drew a slender knife from her belt and peeled off some oak bark. With winter coming it was a useful item to have nearby, for burning it helped ward off illness and pain.

Moving on, she snipped off cuttings from a lonely fir tree that sat on the edge of the oak thicket. Needles from this tree were used in blessing a mother and her newborn. Morag, Varar's sister, had just given birth, and Ailene wanted to keep both mother and bairn safe. Next she collected cuttings of Blackthorn, Ash, Betony, and Hawthorne, among others. All of these plants had specific properties—from healing and protection, to warding off evil spirits, and defending warriors in battle.

Ailene needed them all.

The light was starting to fade by the time she returned to Balintur. Cresting the final hill before the village, she stopped a moment, her gaze resting upon her destination. The watch had lit braziers atop the stone walls. After a blustery day, the wind had finally died. The men and women who worked the fields all day had returned home as dusk settled over the land.

Ailene heaved a sigh. It was now too dark to help herself to a cabbage. It looked like she would be having oatcakes for supper—again.

Hiking her now heavy basket up on one hip, she continued down the hill to the north gate.

The warriors standing guard greeted her as she approached. Ailene's heart sank when she recognized one of them: Fingal.

The Wolf warrior flashed her a wide grin and stepped forward to block her path. "You're late this eve, Ailene. We've just closed the gates."

Ailene raised her chin slightly, meeting Fingal's eye. Last time they had shared words, he had been angry, threatening even. But now he was back to his brash, teasing self. Even so, she did not trust him.

"I'm sure you'll open them ... for me," she replied, forcing a smile.

"I might, for a kiss."

Ailene stiffened. She really was not in the mood for this. However, she was careful not to let her smile slip. "Did you hear that, Owen?" she called out to the other Wolf warrior guarding the gates. "Fingal is hankering for a kiss ... why don't you give him one?"

Owen, an older man with a weather-beaten face, snorted a laugh. "He won't be getting one from me."

Ailene turned back to Fingal. "Then I suppose I shall be out here all night," she replied. "For you won't be receiving a kiss from me either."

Fingal's grin had faded, and he took a step toward her. "That's not very friendly."

Ailene did not reply. Instead, she cast a pleading look at Owen.

"Enough of this, Fingal," the guard rumbled. "Let the lass pass."

Fingal did not reply for a moment. Instead, he stared at Ailene. Beneath the brashness and aggression, she saw disappointment darken his eyes. He had not forgotten Gateway either it seemed, or forgiven.

"Very well." He stepped back and shouldered the heavy gate open.

Ailene released the breath she had been holding. Thank the Gods, he was not going to be difficult.

However, as she passed by him, Fingal dipped his head close. "But sooner or later, I'm collecting that kiss," he murmured, his voice rough, "and I care not if you give it willingly."

The light faded, taking the buffeting wind with it. Drifting on the smooth surface of the sea, the four companions seated in the boat shared a light supper of oatcakes and sheep's cheese, washed down with apple wine.

A full moon rose to the north-east, hovering above the bulk of the headland they had just rounded: the great Sleat peninsula on The Winged Isle's southern extremity. They were deep in Boar lands now but still some distance from An Teanga.

"Do you want to bring the boat aground?" Fina asked Varar as she brushed crumbs off her lap. "We can press on in the morning."

Varar shook his head. The hoary light of the moon reflected off the arrogant planes of his face, glinting off his tiny hoop earring. "We're safer under the cover of darkness," he pointed out. "If we follow the coastline east, we should reach the fort before dawn ... we'll be able to get closer to it that way."

Listening to The Boar chieftain, Muin felt fatigue press down upon him, warring with the tension that rippled through his body. Of course, Varar's words made sense. They were much easier to spot in daylight, especially once they rowed closer to An Teanga.

However, after traveling all day, his back and shoulders ached. Even taking turns at rowing, he was done in.

Varar was tired too; Muin could see the lines of fatigue on his face. Yet, if *he* was not going to rest, none of them would.

Fina did not reply, although Muin imagined she was as exhausted as the rest of them.

"Very well," Talor replied, his tone resigned. However, Muin noted that his shoulders were tense. Like his companions, Talor was preparing himself for their arrival at their destination. He took one final swig from the wine bladder before stoppering it. "We'd better get moving then." He picked up the oars, his fingers flexing around the smooth wooden surface. Talor then glanced over his shoulder at where Muin perched behind him. "Ready?"

Muin heaved in a deep breath and picked up the oars. Luckily, his hands were already calloused from sword practice and hard labor. Even so, the tendons in his fingers protested as he tightened them around the oars. "Aye, let's go."

The cousins resumed their rowing, the rhythmic splash the only sound in the clear, still night. The water gleamed like oil in the moonlight.

The wind, although wearing, had cooled their skin on the journey south. Now, without it, sweat trickled down Muin's face and neck.

Even so, he enjoyed rowing, for it helped burn off the nervous excitement that bubbled up inside him with each furlong that they inched closer to An Teanga. It was the same sensation that built before battle, one that dissolved the moment he unsheathed his sword and rushed at the enemy. He could sense the building tension in all his companions, despite that conversation had ceased for the present.

They had been traveling for a while, before Varar spoke up again. "An Teanga sits at the end of a wide sound." He kept his voice low, yet it seemed to carry in the stillness. "The broch itself has a clear view in every direction for many furlongs distant. It'll be impossible to get close in daylight."

"So how do we get near enough to spy on their defenses?" Muin asked. "The enemy will have sentries patrolling the land around the fort."

"We'll be invisible enough before sunrise, as long as they don't hear the splash of our oars. We should be able to get close to the broch," Varar replied. "But once dawn breaks, we'll need to find somewhere to hide across the water from the fort."

"You want us to row up to the broch?" Fina asked, an edge to her voice. "Are you sure that's wise?"

"No," Varar growled, "but do you have a better idea?"

"I do," Talor replied before Fina could bite back. His voice was strained as he continued to row. "I suggest we keep back from the fort, find somewhere to hide, and scout out the land once dawn breaks."

"I'll do the scouting," Fina replied quickly.

"Wait." Varar's tone sharpened. "I'm leading this mission, wife. I'll decide who risks their neck."

"I'm the obvious choice, *husband*," Fina countered, not remotely cowed by Varar's stern tone. Instead, Muin heard the anticipation in her voice. She loved scouting missions.

Listening to them, Muin's mouth curved. Varar mac Urcal had met his match in Fina. She bowed before no man and never would. Even so, he tensed at the thought of his cousin putting herself at risk. She could be reckless at times.

"I'm small and quick, and can hide my tracks better than the rest of you." Fina pointed out. "And, I know An Teanga well enough."

Muin suppressed a snort. Of course she did. Fina had been Varar's prisoner just a few months earlier. How quickly things could change. Varar and Fina had once been mortal enemies. She had loathed the man then, but now they were wed.

Fina's pointed words were not lost on Varar. "Very well," he replied, although his tone was rough with disapproval. "But you'd better not let them see you."

Fina's grin flashed white in the moonlight. "Don't worry … I won't."

Ailene walked through the mist.

It was as thick as porridge, so dense that when she stretched out her hand, it disappeared.

Cold, damp air kissed her skin, and nearby a crow cawed.

The coarse croak made foreboding pebble across Ailene's skin. She had never liked crows, with their beady eyes and sharp beaks. Among her people the crow was an omen of death. The bird straddled the worlds of the living and the dead and was often seen as a messenger between the two. The crow symbol carved onto her telling bones was one that she dreaded.

Ailene's breathing quickened.

Death was in the air.

Before her, the mist cleared. A row of cairns appeared, fresh mounds of earth silhouetted against a gloomy sky. A crowd of mourners were gathered before one, lonely figures clad in dark hooded cloaks.

Ailene walked toward them, her feet dragging.

She had attended too many burials in her life. She had grown to dread them.

A woman's voice split the chill silence, soulful and sad.

Ailene's step faltered. It was Tea, Galan's wife. She was singing a lament.

Heart pounding now, Ailene resumed her path toward the cairns. Tea stood nearest, a tall figure before a bier. Her proud face was tilted up to the heavens as she sang; tears streaked her cheeks.

Ailene stopped breathing.

Tea rarely wept. Who lay on the bier behind her?

She wanted to turn then and flee back through the curling mist, and yet it was as if a string was tied around her waist. It pulled her forward, step by step, closer to the burial mound. The doorway yawned open, waiting to receive the body of the dead.

Tea sang on, but none of the words made sense to Ailene. It was as if the woman spoke another tongue. However, the grief in her voice was unmistakable. One of her kin lay dead at her feet.

The crowd parted then, admitting Ailene into their midst.

She did not want to look at the body upon the bier, and yet Ailene knew she must.

They *wanted* her to look.

Her gaze settled upon the tall, bulky figure of Muin mac Galan.

The warrior was dressed in a black leather vest and breeches, his feet bare. Muin's face was ashen, his expression grave in death. His chalk-white hands were clasped over the hilt of the sword that lay upon his torso.

"No!"

Heart pounding, Ailene sat up.

For a moment she was not sure where she was, and then she remembered.

She was in her hut, in Balintur—and she had just awoken from a terrible dream.

"Gods," she whispered, raising a shaking hand to her face. Darkness surrounded her. She slept naked, yet sweat slid down between her breasts and shoulder blades.

Dread prickled her skin, making her shiver.

Ruith had told her of such dreams, yet until now Ailene had never experienced one.

Trembling, she wrapped a fur around her and rose to her feet, padding over to the fire pit in the center of her dwelling. The peat still glowed there, so she grabbed a poker and stirred the embers before adding another fresh lump of peat to the fire. It started to smoke before flaming to life, filling the interior of her hut with light.

Ailene let out a ragged breath.

She did not want to sit in the dark, not after such a terrible dream.

But as she sat there, and her heart slowly steadied, fear cramped her belly.

Once again she wished Ruith was alive to talk to. She needed guidance.

And yet she knew herself it was not a dream like others.

Dreams were not usually so vivid, so clear. It was as if she had stepped into another time.

Ailene shuddered and pulled the furs closer still.

Try as she might to deny it, she knew it was a vision rather than a dream she had just seen.

She had just caught a glimpse of the future.

Chapter Eight
Blood Will Soak the Earth

Dun Ringill
Territory of The Serpent

CATHAL MAC CALUM did not want to visit the bandruí.

The crone lived outside the walls of the fort. He had been displeased to learn that the seer had shunned the safety of Dun Ringill's stone walls in favor of a cave—but no one questioned Old Murdina. If she wanted to dwell in such a place, the choice was hers. The bandruí had always preferred to live apart from folk, even back on the mainland.

Cathal drew his fur mantle close around him, head bent against the gusting wind, and crunched down the pebbly shore. The stone bulk of Dun Ringill rose at his back against a stormy sky. The wind brought spots of rain with it.

The mouth of the cave loomed ahead. It sat well back from the tideline, safe enough from high seas.

Climbing up over seaweed-covered rocks, The Serpent chieftain approached the entrance to the cave. A brazier burned there, and Cathal inhaled the cool scent of burning mint. Bandruís used the herb to cleanse the air.

"Murdina," he called out. "It is I ... Cathal."

A low laugh greeted him. "Of course it is ... enter then."

Blinking, as his eyes adjusted to the dim light, Cathal walked inside. He scanned the murky interior and focused his attention upon the bent figure seated beside a glowing fire pit.

Pale eyes glinted, fixing upon him in a way that made misgiving crawl down Cathal's spine.

He had never liked Old Murdina. The only reason he tolerated her all these years was because she was Lena's great aunt. His wife had adored the crone, had followed her advice in all matters. After Lena's death, nearly a year earlier, Cathal had been tempted to cast the bandruí out, yet he had not acted on the instinct.

Murdina was respected, and feared, by his people. He would not risk her cursing them all.

Even so, the sight of her cunning, wrinkled face, her sly smoke-grey eyes, made his hackles rise.

The crone knew he disliked her.

"I was wondering when you'd pay me a visit, Cathal," Murdina spoke. She had a low, rasping voice that reminded Cathal of a crow's caw. Just another reason why the woman unnerved him.

"I've been busy," he grunted, approaching the fire pit. A low stool sat there, awaiting visitors. Cathal took it without being asked to sit.

"So I've seen." The crone peered at him, her gaze narrowing. "But it is more than that. You took your son's death ill ... you've grown leaner, and I see the lines of grief upon your face."

Cathal tensed. His first-born, Dunchadh, had fallen during the siege of Balintur three moons earlier. The black dog of sorrow, which he had only recently driven off after the loss of Lena, had returned to snap at his heels.

The days following Dunchadh's death had been bleak indeed. Cathal had raged, had blamed the remaining members of his family—his son Tamhas in particular, and even his beloved daughter Mor—for the disaster at Balintur. The village should never have fallen. Once his fury toward his remaining son had burned out, he had turned it outward.

The tribes of this isle would pay for Dunchadh's death. Cathal had arrived upon An t-Eilean Sgitheanach—The Winged Isle—with no rancor toward its people. Of course, they were never going to meekly step aside and let the Cruthini take their lands. However, they had been harder to crush than he had expected.

Some days his thoughts about the revenge he would exact upon the four chieftains who led their people against him made his belly ache.

His stomach burned now as he met the bandruí's eye. "The bitter season is almost upon us," he rumbled, deliberately avoiding discussing Dunchadh. "I need to know what the coming months will bring."

Murdina's wrinkled face grew intense. "Have you had any contact with the enemy?"

Cathal shook his head.

"No demands or threats?"

"None," Cathal replied. "I suspect they're rebuilding their strength so that they can attack in the spring."

Murdina gave a cackle. It was then that Cathal saw that he had interrupted her in the midst of making a necklace. A pile of small bones—most likely from fish, birds, and rodents, lay upon her lap. She was threading them onto a piece of leather.

Cathal frowned. Dressed in a long sleeve-less plaid tunic, the seer was weighed down by bone jewelry: necklaces, bracelets, and even a belt made of bone around her thin waist. He did not see that she needed more of the macabre adornments. Yet the old woman said that the bones spoke to her, advised her.

"Your enemies probably think the same of you," she pointed out, favoring him with a gap-toothed grin. "They will be imagining you here ... licking your wounds while you shore up your defenses."

Cathal clenched his jaw. He did not appreciate the mocking edge to the bandruí's voice. She had always been kind, reverent even, to Lena. Yet with Cathal, the woman was often goading when he spoke to her.

When the isle is mine, I'm ridding myself of this bitch.

"I came here for news of what the future holds," he growled. "Not your opinions."

Murdina's grin faded, and he saw irritation flare in those pale eyes. The bandruí didn't like it when he was rude to her. Cathal cared not for her hurt feelings though.

"What do the birds tell you?" he pressed, leaning forward.

The seer sniffed, her gaze dropping to the bones on her lap. She then picked up a piece and threaded it onto her necklace.

"There were few wrens upon this isle when we arrived in summer," she said eventually, her voice sullen, "and none now they have flown south."

"But what of the crows ... the eagles?"

Her mouth pursed. "The birds of prey are loyal to the folk of this isle, they give me nothing." She threaded another piece of bone onto her necklace before continuing. "The crows speak of death, but that's no surprise ... they croak of nothing else."

Irritation pulsed within Cathal at this news. "I need more than that, Murdina."

The seer glanced up, her gnarled hands pausing in their work. "I can do a divination from the clouds?"

"Go on then."

With a heavy sigh, the old woman put her necklace to one side and rose to her feet. Her bone jewelry rattled as she moved. She was small, so frail these days she appeared birdlike. However, Cathal was not fooled by her appearance. Murdina was tougher than most of his battle-hardened warriors.

Retrieving a wand made of yew from the corner of her cave, the seer padded barefoot toward the entrance. "Come, Cathal."

Ignoring that the woman had just addressed him as if he were a dog, the chieftain stood up and followed her out into daylight.

Despite that the day was cold and grey, the sunlight still stung Cathal's eyes after the dimness within the cave. He stopped a few feet behind the bandruí, watching as she scratched symbols into the dirt in front of her. The yew wand bore scratches, lines that she added to with each passing season. Before her she drew the symbol of the serpent, and then scratched out lines, some straight, some curving, around it.

Cathal remained silent. He knew from previous experience that Murdina hated to be interrupted during divinations. As he looked on, the seer raised her face to the heavens, her eyes closing. She then started to chant, muttering words under her breath that the wind tore away before they reached Cathal.

Long moments passed, and then the bandruí opened her eyes, her gaze scanning the sky.

Cathal also focused his attention upon the heavens. It was a wild sky; racing dark clouds boiled overhead. Surely, the seer would be able to divine much from it. The chieftain's breathing quickened as he waited. He was impatient for news. The need to take action burned within him.

Eventually, Murdina dropped her gaze from the sky and turned to him.

The stern look on her face made Cathal grow still. "What is it?" he demanded. "What did you see?"

"Contradictory things," the bandruí admitted, her fingers tightening around her wand. "Strange things."

"Such as?"

The seer moved toward him, her bones rattling. "There will be conflict soon ... before spring," she replied. Outdoors, the daylight highlighted the web of lines that crisscrossed her face. Cathal was not sure how old the woman was, although she had been the tribe's seer ever since his father's time.

Cathal's brows knitted together. "Will they attack Dun Ringill?"

Murdina let out an irritated sigh. "The clouds cannot give me details such as that. They only hint at what will come."

"And what are they *hinting* at, exactly?" Cathal demanded between gritted teeth.

How he wished Lena was at his side. It had always been her role to visit the bandruí. Murdina had been more forthcoming with the chieftain's wife.

"The balance of power is shifting," the seer replied, her gaze never leaving his face. "Blood will soak the earth before Mid-Winter Fire." She paused there. "You must decide whether you move first, or let the united tribes of this isle come to you."

Cathal's nostrils flared. That was a discussion he needed to have with his warriors back at the broch. Frustration exploded within him, and he was suddenly seized by the urge to be elsewhere.

"Thank you, seer," he grunted, stepping around her. "I will think on this."

A bony hand shot out, gnarled fingers studded with iron and bone rings fastening around his forearm. "Wait," the bandruí croaked. "There is more."

Cathal stiffened. Reluctantly, he turned to Murdina. "Tell it then."

They were standing so close that the crone had to crane her neck up to meet his gaze. She smelled musty, of age and dried herbs. "The clouds held a warning," Murdina said, her voice lowering. "Someone will betray you, Cathal ... someone in your inner circle."

Cathal stared down at her, his body tensing further. "Who?"

"The clouds do not say."

"For the love of the Gods, woman," Cathal exploded. "What use are you to me, if you cannot give me details."

Murdina released his arm and stepped back, her grey eyes hooding. "I don't exist to serve you, chieftain," she replied, her voice a low rasp. "I'm merely a conduit between this world and the next ... and I have given you much to think on." She turned to go then, heading back toward the cave. However, before disappearing inside, the bandruí turned and cast Cathal a cold look over her shoulder. "Watch your back ... for someone you love is whetting their blade and awaiting their chance."

Chapter Nine

Occupied Territory

An Teanga
Territory of The Serpent

MUIN PEERED ACROSS the water, at where the outline of the broch of An Teanga rose against a backdrop of velvet green hills. "Fina should be back by now," he murmured, frowning. "Where's she got to?"

Next to him, Talor shifted while Varar remained still. The three of them crouched behind a large boulder by the water's edge. It was the closest they could safely get to their destination without risking being spotted. They had hidden their boat out of sight in the trees behind them just before dawn, and then Fina had crept off to investigate further.

However, the sun was high in the sky now—and Muin's fiery cousin had not yet reappeared.

"I should go after her," Talor muttered under his breath. "She's taking too long."

"If anyone goes after Fina, it'll be me," Varar growled, a warning in his voice. "And would the pair of you stop worrying. I wouldn't have let her go if I didn't think she was the best person for the task."

Talor cast Varar a dark look in reply, while Muin's mouth thinned. Fina was like a sister to him and Talor; and despite her prowess as a warrior, they both tended to be overprotective of her.

Varar, it seemed, was more inclined to trust in her abilities.

"Keep your voices down." An irritated female whisper reached them then. "Sound carries across the water." A moment later a small figure emerged from the broom bushes to the left of the boulder.

Fina.

A slow smile stretched across Varar's face as he turned to face his wife. "I was just reassuring these two that you were on your way back."

Fina grinned before sinking to her haunches behind the boulder. A light sheen of sweat covered her golden skin, her cheeks were flushed, and she was breathing fast. "Good to know someone thinks I'm capable of spying on the enemy without getting caught," she replied.

Talor snorted, but Muin's swift elbow to the ribs stopped him from commenting further.

"What did you discover?" Varar asked, his face growing serious.

Fina wiped her brow with the back of her hand before answering. "It was difficult to get close to the broch," she admitted. "They've got sentries everywhere. I nearly got spotted twice." Fina paused here, the confidence ebbing from her face. "There were more of them than I thought," she admitted. "I thought I was going to have to kill one ... but luckily he didn't see me sneak past."

Muin frowned. "Killing sentries won't help us. How many are defending the fort?"

"Difficult to tell ... but I'd say at least two-hundred warriors."

Muin exhaled sharply. He had hoped the garrison at An Teanga would be far smaller than that.

"Where are they guarding?" Varar asked. His body had gone still as he took in his wife's news.

"There's one posted every few yards around the base of the broch, keeping watch on the water," Fina replied. "It's just as well we didn't try to bring the boat in closer." She paused there, her brow furrowing. "They've also posted sentries at the gates leading from the village to the broch, and along the entire perimeter of the village itself."

"Any sentries farther out?" Muin asked.

Fina nodded. "Like I said, they're thick on the ground. I saw a number on the eastern and western approaches."

Talor huffed out a breath at this news. "Well then ... at least we know what we're facing."

Varar's face tightened at that. "We can take two-hundred of them ... with everyone's help."

Talor frowned. "Aye, but won't it leave Balintur undefended?"

Muin tensed. His cousin had a point.

Varar twisted round, meeting Talor's eye. "More warriors from The Wolf and The Stag are joining us at Balintur," he pointed out. "There will be enough to take back An Teanga *and* defend the north ... there has to be."

Rain was lashing across Balintur when Varar's party returned. Dusk settled in a grey, wet blanket over the land.

Muin followed his companions over the exposed hills that led to the valley where the village nestled. The rain drove in from the north, stinging needles of ice that peppered the exposed skin of his face and arms.

None of the party spoke. They were all too weary and chilled to converse, focused instead on the warm cups of mead and hot meals that awaited them at their destination.

Head bowed, Muin strode on, cresting the last hill before Balintur. And with each footstep, tension grew in the pit of his belly.

Muin had been glad of this mission, had enjoyed being focused on something beyond himself. Over the last day, his thoughts had been on sneaking close to An Teanga, and on getting the information they needed on its defense before getting out of occupied territory.

But now it was done, he was forced to face what awaited him in Balintur.

Ailene.

He was also grateful for the foul weather, for it kept most folk indoors. Those who worked the fields had retreated within the village walls, and the guards at the south gate looked miserable, hunched under oilskin capes. Hopefully, Ailene would be at home too, sheltering from the rain like everyone else.

Muin was not in the mood to face the seer.

Grow a spine, man, he chided himself. *You knew the risks when you poured your heart out to her.*

Aye, he had—but it did not make rejection any easier. Disappointment was a knife to the guts, and the pain had not eased over the past two days as he had hoped.

But it did not matter how humiliated and hurt he was, Balintur was too small for him to avoid the bandruí forever. Folk would notice for one thing, for Ailene and Muin spent a lot of time together usually.

The only way he was going to get through this was to bury his feelings deep and put on a face. He would have to pretend he did not care, no matter what it cost him.

Once they passed through the gates, Varar led them straight to the meeting house in the heart of the village.

Muin's heart sank. He had hoped for a brief reprieve, before they met with everyone.

Ailene would join the chieftains. She never missed a council.

Enough. Anger curled up within Muin—at himself. *This won't do.* It was time to build a shield, one no one—especially Ailene—could penetrate.

It was time to construct a wall around his heart.

Ailene ducked into the meeting house and shook the rain off her hair and cloak. The interior of the house was warm and smelled of peat-smoke and wet plaid and leather.

Her gaze shifted over those gathered. The chieftains and their kin were already there, as were the four who had returned from the scouting party. The latter were huddled around the fire pit. There were few smiles inside the meeting house, as those present anxiously awaited the scouting party's news.

Ailene shared their nervousness. Much depended on taking An Teanga back successfully.

Although she had told herself that she would act normally and focus on the council itself, Ailene's gaze settled upon Muin. His long dark hair was wet and slicked back off his face; the rain had also soaked through the leather vest and breeches he wore. His grey eyes were introspective as he stared into the fire. He held his hands out, warming them over the glowing lumps of peat.

Relief filtered through Ailene at the sight of him, the sensation so strong that her legs suddenly felt weak. That dream had shadowed her all day. She had felt sick with worry until Eara ran to her hut to inform her that the scouting party had returned.

Gods, she had never been so pleased to be proved wrong. Maybe that vision had not been a premonition after all, just a bad dream.

"Ailene!" Fina called out and beckoned her over. She sat next to Varar, who had an arm slung protectively over her shoulders. Morag had joined them for this meeting, her baby son nestled against her breast in a sling. Morag's strong face was strained as she awaited her brother's news.

Muin did glance up then, although his face was expressionless when he looked at Ailene.

Her belly tightened in response. She had hoped nothing would change between them, but the aloofness in his eyes told her otherwise.

Favoring Fina with a tight smile, Ailene approached the fire. "Glad to see you all back safely," she greeted them.

"It's good to be back ... we almost froze to death on the journey home," Talor grumbled. "That wind was like The Reaper's breath." Indeed, her cousin was pale with cold, his broad shoulders hunched as he inched closer to the fire.

"Here you go." Tea approached, carrying a tray of steaming cups. Ailene caught the sweet scent of mead. "Something to warm you up."

"Thanks, Ma." Muin took a cup, a small smile gracing his lips as he met his mother's eye.

The sight of the warmth on his face made the knot in Ailene's belly grow tighter. Hurt flooded through her. He had a smile for his mother, but not for his oldest friend.

"Never mind whining on about the cold." Muin's brother, Aaron, had swaggered up and now stood next to his mother, arms folded across his chest. His handsome face was tense with irritation. "Surely you've got more to share with us than that?"

Talor favored his cousin with a sour look. "Aye ... with the *chieftains*, not with you."

Aaron snorted, before he flipped Talor an obscene gesture. Although Talor and Muin had always gotten on, Muin's younger brother had started to butt heads with his older cousin of late. Ailene supposed it was because the two of them were similarly bull-headed and outspoken.

"Aaron," Tea reprimanded her son, her tone sharp. "Mind your manners."

"We're ready." Galan's voice cut through the rumble of conversation. The Eagle chieftain had taken a seat and was watching Varar intently, his grey eyes shadowed with worry. "Aaron isn't the only one interested to hear how your mission went."

Chapter Ten
Raising Concerns

GALAN FROWNED, THE expression turning his face severe. "I didn't think they would have left such a large force at An Teanga."

Across the fire, Varar continued to hold The Eagle chieftain's eye. "We can take them." He broke off then, his attention shifting to where the leader of The Wolf, Wid, sat silently listening. "When will your warriors get here?"

"Within the next day or two," Wid replied. His bearded face was stern.

"As will more of The Stag," Tadhg spoke up. "I've called up warriors from every corner of my territory for this ... we have barely enough to defend Dun Grianan now."

"Your stronghold is safe," Galan assured him.

Tadhg's brow furrowed. "You can't know that for sure, Galan."

An awkward silence fell in the meeting house.

Muin shifted on his stool, his fingers flexing around the cup of mead. The drink had warmed his belly and taken the chill out of his limbs, yet the tension inside the meeting house put him on edge. He had sensed it from the moment he stepped inside. The three chieftains who had remained behind at Balintur were all quieter than usual, their gazes shuttered as they listened to Varar's report.

For decades the four tribes of this isle—The Eagle, The Wolf, The Stag, and The Boar—had endured long periods of conflict. It was a rare thing indeed, to see all the chieftains seated around a fire together, uniting against a common enemy.

However, the air was now charged, warning Muin that the peace between them was still a fragile thing. The tension made him forget his own personal disappointments, his discomfort regarding Ailene.

These men had to remain united, but at the same time they had to make the right decision. The future of all the peoples depended upon it.

"Once the rest of The Wolf and Stag warriors arrive, we will be able to move on An Teanga," Varar said finally. "We will ensure a force is left here in Balintur ... we'll not leave this village undefended."

"Is taking back An Teanga really the best course of action?" Tadhg's blue eyes shadowed. "Dun Ringill is where The Serpent leader dwells. Isn't that a wiser target?"

"You heard the bandruí at our last meeting," Galan replied, scowling. "Fortune shines upon The Boar at present ... but not The Eagle. We would be fools to go against such advice."

All gazes swiveled to where Ailene sat at the edge of the group.

Ailene stared back at the chieftains. She sat proudly upon her stool although Muin knew her well enough to see the tension in her shoulders, the strain upon her face.

"Are you still convinced of what the bones foresaw?" Tadhg asked.

Ailene nodded. "Aye," she replied. There was no doubt on her face or in her tone. "I cast them again yesterday, and nothing has changed."

A few feet away, Wid let out a long sigh. "I'm not sure we should blindly trust the word of such a young bandruí," he rumbled. The Wolf chieftain's gaze fixed upon Ailene. "No offense, lass ... but even old and wise seers have been known to divine things wrongly."

Muin watched Ailene's spine go rigid. Her sea-blue eyes darkened, and her jaw tightened.

"I trust Ailene," Galan cut in. "She has not steered us wrong yet. If she thinks we should wait before taking back Dun Ringill, I will heed her."

A nerve flickered under one of Ailene's eyes at this proclamation, and she shot Galan a look of gratitude.

Muin shifted uncomfortably on his stool. Unlike Wid, he trusted in Ailene's predictions. However, he also shared Tadhg's concerns about taking back An Teanga rather than Dun Ringill. Muin's gut intuition told him they should focus on The Eagle stronghold.

"We will need a large force to take back An Teanga," Muin spoke up then. "Even with more warriors in place here in Balintur, we're spreading ourselves too thin."

Unease rippled around the fireside. Fina scowled at him, irritation kindling in her grey eyes, while Varar frowned. Talor, however, nodded.

Galan had gone still. "And what would you have us do, son?" he asked. Next to The Eagle chief, Aaron was staring at his older brother, a quizzical expression upon his face.

Muin inhaled deeply. Of course Aaron was surprised. Muin rarely publically disagreed with his father. He was not sure why he felt the need to do so now, only that he was tired of holding his tongue for fear of disappointing his father. Ailene's rejection had changed him, freeing him of his usual reserve. In future, he intended to speak his mind in these councils.

Ailene was watching him now, her brow furrowed. Ignoring her, Muin held his father's gaze. "I think we should gather our full force and hit Dun Ringill hard," he said quietly. "Before Mid-Winter Fire."

"That's too risky," Galan replied, negating the suggestion with a curt shake of his head. "There are hundreds of The Serpent residing in the fort now ... they could hold out for a long time."

"And meanwhile, we'd freeze once the snows came," Varar added. "Even with two-hundred warriors defending An Teanga, it will be easier to take back than Dun Ringill. The Eagle fort needs to wait till spring."

"And what will happen when Cathal mac Calum hears of the attack?" Talor asked. "Will he just sit there and let us drive his people out of Boar territory?"

Varar's mouth twisted. "If we move fast, by the time he learns of it, nothing he does will matter ... we will have taken back An Teanga."

Talor frowned. "Meanwhile, Balintur will still be exposed."

"We have rebuilt and strengthened this village's defenses," Galan pointed out, a warning edge to his tone now. "And with the arrival of the extra warriors there will be plenty of us to defend it." Muin sensed his father's rising irritation. He did not like that his son and nephew were being so forceful in their opinions, especially with the other three chieftains present. Muin felt his own temper simmer in response; a strange sensation, for he hardly ever quarreled with his father.

Muin sometimes felt as if his father did not want to hear his opinion. Galan wanted to be followed, not questioned. He seemed to forget that his first-born son had reached manhood many years earlier and already fought in a number of battles.

Another silence settled around the fireside, this one even more charged than previously.

"I think," Ailene spoke up, shattering the growing sense of disquiet, "that it would be best you all think on this before making a decision. Much depends upon your choice."

Galan shook his head, his jaw setting in a stubborn expression that Muin knew well. His father was even-tempered and fair-minded, yet he had an obstinate streak when angered.

"Time is running out for us all," he replied. "We can't sit around arguing ... a decision has to be made."

"I agree," Fina said, her expression the grimmest Muin had seen it in a long while. "Enough talk."

Wid huffed, sitting back and massaging a muscle in his shoulder. "Come on then ... the chieftains should all cast a vote. Those in favor of taking back An Teanga first, stand up."

Varar rose to his feet first, and then Galan. All gazes in the meeting house then shifted to Wid and Tadhg.

The Stag chieftain crossed brawny arms across a muscular chest but remained seated, making it clear that he did not agree with Galan's plan. Tadhg's response both pleased and surprised Muin. Others shared his concerns, it seemed.

The deciding vote lay with Wid.

Realizing this, The Wolf chieftain muttered a curse under his breath. He then shared a long look with his wife Alana. Glowering, he slowly heaved himself off his stool.

Muin let out the breath he was holding, disappointment filtering through him. He had hoped that Wid would stand against Galan and Varar on this. He could see that the man was torn, but in the end he had given in to pressure that had nothing to do with the decision at hand. Galan and Tea's handfasting many years earlier had brought an end to decades of feuding between The Wolf and The Eagle. Wid was wary of dredging up old animosities again.

"It's decided then," Galan said, his gaze sweeping over the faces of those gathered around the fire pit. Muin tensed when his father's attention settled upon him. He was daring him to open his mouth again, to stir up trouble. "We will move against An Teanga ... and soon."

Muin strode from the meeting house and had barely gone three paces when Fina caught up with him.

"What was that about?" she rounded on him, blocking his path.

The rain still slashed across the village, tugging at their clothing and hair. However, Fina barely seemed to notice. In the light of the guttering pitch torches surrounding the meeting house, her beautiful face was livid. Viewing his cousin's rigid stance, the way her hands balled into fists by her sides, Muin realized he had angered more than his father this evening.

"I was just raising my concerns," he replied evenly. "Shouldn't I have done?"

"You said nothing to any of us on the journey back from An Teanga."

"That's because I wanted to think upon it first." Muin frowned then. "Surely you can see why I'm worried?"

Fina's full mouth thinned. "No."

Muin inclined his head. "You're blinkered these days, Fina."

"Excuse me?"

"Now you're wed to Varar, your priorities have changed."

His cousin's nostrils flared. "How dare you ... I'm still an Eagle. I care about my people's welfare just as much as you do."

"I don't doubt that," Muin countered. "But you also want to see your husband take back his fort ... no matter what the cost."

Fina took an aggressive step toward him, and for a moment Muin thought she might lash out. In all their years growing up together, the pair of them had never argued like this. Muin was always the level-headed one, the person who broke up fights but never started them.

But this evening he felt the urge to tangle horns with anyone who crossed him, and that included his feisty cousin.

"I don't know what's amiss with you at the moment," Fina growled. "But I don't like it."

"There's nothing wrong," Muin struck back, his own anger simmering now. "I'm just tired of staying silent when I wish to voice my opinions. You've never had difficulty speaking your mind ... why shouldn't the rest of us say what we think?"

Muin left his fuming cousin and wandered the web of narrow dirt lanes, making his way back to the dwelling that he and Talor shared.

Night had fallen in a grey, wet shroud. The rain was driving in horizontally now, and despite the fur mantle around his shoulders, Muin shivered. The fire and a cup of warm mead had thawed his limbs a little, although the conversation inside the meeting house had darkened Muin's mood.

He did not like arguing with those he loved.

He did not like making a scene or displeasing his father.

But he shared Talor and Tadhg's views, and he would not hold his tongue, even if it meant making himself unpopular.

"Muin!"

A familiar female voice hailed him—not Fina this time but someone he wanted to see even less.

Ailene.

Cursing under his breath, Muin halted and turned to face the cloaked figure that hurried toward him.

Realizing that he had stopped, the seer halted, her feet slipping in the mud.

A moment later she careened into Muin.

Chapter Eleven

Mutton Stew

MUIN'S ARMS FASTENED around Ailene, just as she nearly fell over. He hauled her upright, and the feel of her warmth and softness caused his breathing to hitch. When he was sure she was not going to slip into the mud, Muin stepped back so that their bodies were no longer touching.

He almost pushed her away from him in his haste to get some distance.

"What is it, Ailene?" He was aware that his voice held a harsh edge, yet he did not soften it. "I've been traveling all day ... I'm tired."

Breathing hard, Ailene withdrew and pushed back the cowl of her cloak so that their gazes met properly.

Her eyes gleamed, although not from hurt or tears, but anger. "What's wrong with you?" she demanded.

Muin tensed, his own temper kindling. First Fina and now Ailene—he was tired of women taking bites out of his hide this evening. "Leave it, Ally," he growled. "Now isn't the time."

They stared at each other, although Ailene did not back away. Moments passed while the wind howled and the rain sliced into them. "I'm not leaving it," she replied finally. "Is this how it'll be from now on ... you sulking ... pretending I don't exist?"

Muin folded his arms across his chest, his brow furrowing. She made him sound like a petulant child. "Of course not."

"Then, it's time we mended things." She took a step toward him, clutching at her sodden cloak as another squall washed over them. "Come on ... let's get out of this foul weather."

Muin hesitated, frustration pulsing through him. Ailene did not seem to understand. The hurt of her rejection was still an open wound. It physically hurt to be near this woman.

"I've made mutton stew," she added hopefully.

Muin huffed out a breath, hesitating. He pushed his wet hair off his face as a particularly heavy gust pummeled them. Of course there was nothing he wanted more than to spend the evening with Ailene, listening to the lilt of her voice as she cooked for them. And yet being in her presence was torture. Did she not realize that?

He could not forget what had happened last time he visited her hut. It would always lie between them now, souring their once easy rapport.

"Muin?" Hurt flashed in Ailene's blue eyes.

"Very well," he muttered. "Let's go."

Muin followed Ailene to her hut, misgiving dogging his steps.

Spending time with her in his current mood was not wise, and yet he found it impossible to deny her. Despite his disappointment and soreness at being rejected, he still did not want to hurt Ailene.

Ducking inside out of the rain, Muin inhaled the aroma of mutton stew. An iron pot bubbled over the fire pit. The air inside Ailene's dwelling was warm and dry. Muin rose to his full height, shook the rain from his hair, and shrugged off his sodden mantle, hanging it up behind the door. Ailene passed him her cloak, and he pegged it up next to his before crossing to the fire pit.

The warmth of the glowing peat suffused his body, chasing away the chill, and Muin held out his numbed fingers toward it.

"I'm making dumplings to go with the stew," Ailene announced, busying herself at her long work table. "I know you like them."

Muin's belly growled in answer, even before he had time to reply, and Ailene cast him a smile over her shoulder. "You must be starving?"

Muin grimaced. "I haven't eaten a decent meal in two days," he admitted.

His gaze followed Ailene as she prepared the dumplings: mixing ground oats with lard, herbs, and milk. She had taken off her dirty boots and padded about barefoot on the dirt floor. Her long plaid skirt was damp, its hem edged with mud, and water still gleamed off the bare skin of her arms. Her hair hung in wild, wet curls down her back.

She had never looked so beautiful.

Throat constricting, Muin dragged his gaze from Ailene and stared into the fire. Gods, how he wanted her. It was no good. It had been a mistake to agree to supper. Time would perhaps heal all wounds, but tonight his guts were still in knots, and his chest ached.

Ailene approached the fire pit then, with a wooden platter of dumplings, which she dropped into the bubbling stew.

Muin's mouth watered at the sight of them. Despite his churning belly, he had not lied. He was so hungry he felt light-headed.

"Some mead?" Ailene asked.

"Aye," Muin murmured. "Thanks."

She passed him a cup and settled down onto a stool opposite.

An uncomfortable silence fell.

"The dumplings shouldn't take long to cook," Ailene said finally, flashing Muin another smile.

Muin nodded but didn't reply. His quietness was making her uneasy. Beneath her smile, he sensed Ailene's tension. He knew he was being sullen, yet he could not think of a thing to say. His mind was empty, except for a melee of angry, churning thoughts that Ailene did not need to hear.

He took a deep draft of mead, hoping that would relax him. It slaked his thirst, but it did not make him feel any better.

"I always thought you believed in my divinations." Ailene spoke up once more, her expression growing solemn. "Do you think I'm steering everyone wrong?"

Muin dragged in a deep breath. "Of course I don't," he replied.

"But you think we should abandon our plans to attack An Teanga ... and take back Dun Ringill instead?"

"Aye, but that doesn't mean I don't believe the bones."

Her brow furrowed. "You think I'm misreading them?"

Muin shrugged. He knew the gesture was dismissive, yet he could not help himself. "I know you sometimes doubt yourself, Ally."

As soon as the words were out, Muin regretted them. Ailene's expression visibly closed, her blue eyes shuttering.

"I confided in you," she said, her voice hardening. "I told you things I wouldn't breathe to another. Now I wish I hadn't."

Muin's pulse quickened. He wanted to apologize, but something stubborn within prevented him.

Face stony, Ailene rose to her feet then and retrieved two earthen bowls from the table. She roughly ladled out bowls of mutton stew and dumplings, her movements choppy with anger, and handed one to Muin.

He took the bowl, careful not to let his fingers brush hers. Muin shoved a wooden spoon into the stew and dug into a dumpling. It was hot and scalded his mouth, but it was easier to focus on eating rather than the awkward, fraught conversation.

Ailene went quiet, and Muin had devoured half his bowl, before he glanced up and saw that she had not touched her stew. Instead, she was looking at him in a way that made him grow still.

It was the same expression his mother had worn when he had behaved badly as a bairn. Her gaze had narrowed. Her soft mouth had thinned.

"I don't know what's come over you, Muin," she said, her voice low and hard. "But I wish the man I used to know would come back."

Muin left shortly after supper, and Ailene was relieved to see him go.

The door thudded shut behind him, leaving her alone by the fireside. Ailene did not move for a long while.

It had been a mistake to invite Muin to supper, to try and mend things between them. They had both crossed a bridge and burned it behind them; there was no returning to the way things once had been.

She realized that now.

The friendship was indeed ruined.

Muin, who had been so kind and understanding all these years, whom she had confided in about nearly everything, suddenly seemed a surly, confrontational stranger. She could not undo what had been said, or seen.

She would just have to accept it.

Ailene's throat suddenly thickened then, a lump rising. Irritated, she swallowed hard.

Times were bleak for her people, and it looked as if she would have to deal with what would come on her own.

It was odd really—that she should feel lonely. After her parents' deaths the folk of Dun Ringill had rallied around her. She could not have wished for a more loving community.

Yet at the same time, she had always felt an outsider. No surprise really that she had chosen the path of bandruí, a role that would always keep her a little apart from folk.

Don't hide behind your role, Ally. The words of her aunt Ruith came back to her then. The old woman had known of Ailene's tendency to shy away from others. *Don't use it as an excuse to keep those whom love you at bay.*

Was that what she was doing now?

Muin had always been so good to her. He was three years her junior, yet she had never seen him as a little brother. He was her best friend, a 'wise soul', as Ruith had once called him, with a seriousness that belied his years.

Ailene was not blind. She knew that Muin was attractive: tall and strong, with long, dark silky hair. She had noticed other women flirt with him, smiling up at the chieftain's hulking son under fluttering lashes.

Their attempts had once made her smile, for Muin did not revel in the attention the way his cousin Talor did. The first time it had happened, he had blushed like the setting sun, although she had seen he had grown accustomed to female attention over the years. He had even once taken a lover, a comely widow who had since wed again—to someone else.

But Ailene had never been jealous. She had never seen Muin as anything other than a friend.

It did not matter how disappointed he was, she could not help how she felt.

Chapter Twelve

Stubborn

LAUGHTER AND MUSIC greeted Ailene as she wove her way through the crowd. Warriors thronged the wide dirt space in the heart of Balintur, their faces lit by braziers lining the square.

The strains of a harp and a woman's voice filtered through the crisp night air. Eithni and Tea were performing.

The corners of Ailene's mouth lifted. Two days had passed since her supper with Muin, and for the first time since that evening, she felt her heart lighten. As a child she would listen to the sisters perform for the folk of Dun Ringill. Eithni played like a fairy maid, and Tea had a voice to make the Gods weep. They sang a happy, bawdy tune now, one about bountiful harvests and amorous wives and husbands.

This was the last evening before the campaign to take back An Teanga began. Tonight's gathering was a send-off for the army.

Ailene had not felt like attending. A melancholic mood had settled upon her since the scouting party's return; dark shadows dogged her steps. Even so, she had forced herself to leave her warm, safe hut and venture out into the chill, windless evening.

Stopping near the middle of the gathering, Ailene's gaze went to where the two sisters sat upon a wooden platform, performing.

The years had been kind to both Tea and Eithni. Their faces looked alive and youthful as they performed for the crowd. The two women were of The Wolf tribe and had been instrumental in weaving peace between the two peoples. Ailene's mouth curved further. The sisters were as different as night and day: Tea tall, dark, and proud; Eithni small and brown-haired. One was a warrior, the other a healer—and together they had done much to strengthen The Eagle.

Although they were no relation to her, Ailene saw both women much like aunts. Eithni especially had been a good friend of her mother's and had cared for Mael during her illness.

As Ailene looked on, Eithni's slender fingers danced across the harp strings. Her hazel eyes shone with delight as Tea accompanied her, and the surrounding crowd started to clap in time with the song.

Ailene found herself clapping along with them, the heavy mood of the past few days sloughing away.

She had not wanted to join the revelry, but she was glad she had.

Cups of warm mead were being passed around, and Ailene took one gratefully. She wrapped her chilled fingers around the warm wooden cup and continued her path through the throng to where Fina and Talor were deep in conversation. Fina was scowling, while Talor appeared to be trying to convince her of something.

Ailene slowed her step as she approached, unwilling to intrude. However, a moment later, her friend and cousin both spotted her. Fina's scowl disappeared and she smiled, while Talor waved her over.

"I'm glad you came," Fina greeted her. "I was beginning to think I was going to have to drag you out here."

Ailene laughed before raising her cup to her lips and taking a sip of warmed mead. "You almost had to ... I've not felt that sociable of late."

She realized Talor was watching her. Her cousin's sea-blue eyes—the same shade as hers—were narrowed, his face uncharacteristically serious. "Is all well, cousin?" he asked. "The chieftains have asked much of you of late."

"Aye, everything is well," Ailene assured him with a smile. "Don't fret."

"Do you have concerns about the campaign?" Fina asked, her brow furrowing once more.

Ailene shook her head. "I've cast the bones every morning since the decision was made to take back An Teanga ... and nothing has changed. The omens look favorable for The Boar ... less so for The Eagle."

Both Fina and Talor's expressions darkened at this, and Ailene's chest tightened. This was why she had started to avoid folk of late; like a crow upon their shoulders, she felt as if she was a harbinger of doom.

Glancing around, Ailene spotted Muin on the other side of the gathering space. He was speaking to his father, Galan. Standing close, their gazes fused as they talked, Ailene was struck by just how similar father and son were, although they looked like they were arguing.

Seeing the direction of Ailene's gaze, Fina raised an eyebrow. "I know ... it's not something you see often."

Ailene shifted her attention to Fina. "What are they arguing about?"

"Muin has asked the chief to remain in Balintur, while *he* leads The Eagle warriors," Talor replied. "They've been fighting about it for days. Uncle Galan doesn't like the idea."

Ailene glanced back at the two men. Muin was gesticulating now, his dark brows knitted together. Galan, however, looked as immovable as a block of granite. He took a step back from his son, heavily muscled arms folding over his chest.

"I'm not surprised," Ailene murmured. "Galan is proud."

Talor snorted. "It's the way between fathers and sons," he replied. "Da doesn't like it when I question him these days either ... at a certain age the old wolf starts to feel threatened by the cub."

Fina laughed. "Or maybe the cub just needs teaching some manners."

Muin and Galan finished their argument then, with The Eagle chieftain shaking his head, his expression thunderous. Muin turned on his heel and stalked away, heading toward where Talor, Fina, and Ailene stood.

Ailene's belly tightened at the sight of his approach. She had hoped to avoid Muin this evening.

Muin looked intimidating when riled, she noted. Anger turned his features hawkish and deepened his storm grey eyes.

"No luck, I take it?" Talor greeted his cousin with a half-smile.

Muin shook his head before muttering a curse under his breath.

"He won't stay behind and let you lead The Eagle?" Talor asked.

"No ... you and your father are tasked with that."

Talor scowled. "What? I'm staying behind?"

"Aye ... Donnel will rule in my father's stead while we're gone, and you and Tarl will help him."

Talor's expression turned thunderous. "Whose idea was this?"

"Not ours, obviously." There was no mistaking the bitter edge of Muin's voice. "Both our fathers don't trust us to make decisions on our own it seems." He raked a hand through his hair. "I think that all the chieftains, except Varar, should remain at Balintur during the attack. We must keep this village strong. It makes sense to let Varar lead the siege."

"Your father's stubborn," Fina pointed out, a small, wry smile playing upon her lips, "and he likes to be in control."

Muin's mouth twisted. "Aye."

Listening to the conversation, Ailene felt misgiving settle over her. "Are you going to An Teanga?" she asked, addressing Muin for the first time.

Muin met her gaze, his expression shuttered. "Aye ... father wants me and Aaron to fight at his side."

The evening wore on, and drinking and conversation shifted into dancing. Men and women whirled around the heart of the gathering space, hair flying behind them as they clapped, stamped, and twisted in time to the music.

Muin watched from the edge of the crowd, fingers clamped around a cup of untouched mead. It had long since gone cold; he had little appetite for drink this evening.

They would move out at dawn, and he wanted a clear head.

Nearby, Ailene and Fina were deep in conversation, heads bowed together, while Talor was flirting with one of Tadhg mac Fortrenn's daughters. His cousin had been annoyed to discover that he was remaining in Balintur with Donnel, but a few cups of mead had mellowed his mood.

Muin's humor, on the other hand, had only gotten darker.

Frustration churned within him. Not only had his hopes of a future with Ailene been crushed, but his father had made it clear that he did not trust Muin to lead The Eagle warriors into battle.

It was insulting. Muin had proved himself repeatedly of late, but it seemed that Galan wanted his son to follow orders, not give them. He took counsel from his brothers, yet he did not want his son's opinion. The harder Muin had pushed, the more stubborn his father had become.

It was a fight Muin was never going to win.

"Good eve, Muin." A brown-haired woman with warm blue-grey eyes stepped up before him. "It has been a while."

"Gavina." Warmth rushed through Muin as he leaned forward and kissed the woman on the cheek. "How have you been?"

"I'm expecting a bairn," she announced. Indeed, one of her hands splayed across her swelling midriff. She wore a long sleeveless tunic with a fur stole around her shoulders. "It's due just after Bealtunn."

The first genuine smile in days stretched Muin's face. "Congratulations."

Gavina, who had once shown him the ways of the furs, had wed again just over a year earlier. When Muin had come of age, Gavina had just been widowed. Wed to a cruel man, she had been relieved to find herself alone again, and had taken Muin to her furs for a short while.

Muin had been an eager pupil and was disappointed when, after six passion-fueled months, Gavina had ended the affair. She was ten years his elder and wished to wed again. Although they had become close, she had also realized that Muin's heart belonged elsewhere, even then.

A shadow passed over Gavina's face. "Donnan will be going with you to An Teanga," she said softly. "I'd prefer he remain here to help protect Balintur, but Galan has insisted."

Muin tensed. Of course he had. Donnan mac Muir was one of their fiercest warriors. Galan would want him at his side for the siege.

"Will you look out for him, Muin?" Gavina asked. "Make sure he comes back to me safely?"

Muin held her gaze, a smile tugging at his mouth. "Donnan doesn't need protecting," he reminded her. "If anything, The Serpent will fill their breeches at the sight of him."

Gavina gave a shaky laugh, although the shadow never left her eyes. "Even so, I'd feel better knowing you were watching out for him."

Muin's smile faded, before he nodded. "Of course I will." The music changed then, slowing to a mellow, lilting tune. A song for lovers. "Go find Donnan," Muin murmured. "Enjoy your time together."

Watching Gavina walk away, Muin felt an odd pang. He remembered when Donnan had first started showing an interest in the comely widow; Muin had been irritated and jealous initially. But now, three years later, the couple were deeply in love, and he was glad he had stepped aside so they could be together.

Of course, at the time he had hoped for a future with Ailene.

He spotted the seer then, on the other side of the gathering. She had finished her conversation with Fina and now stood apart from the dancers. She looked as if she was about to leave.

A man was preventing her.

Fingal mac Diarmid—The Wolf warrior who had wooed Ailene over the past few months.

However, unlike at Gateway, Ailene did not look pleased to see the warrior. Fingal had hold of her arm and was attempting to haul her into the dancing. Ailene was saying something, her face taut with displeasure.

Muin tensed. It was clear that Ailene did not want to dance.

And then Fingal yanked Ailene against him and tried to kiss her.

Chapter Thirteen

I Can't

AILENE KNEED FINGAL in the cods.

The Wolf warrior sank to his knees, face twisting in anger and pain. But he did not loosen his grip on her arm.

Half a dozen long strides brought Muin across the space and to Ailene's side. She was struggling to free herself from Fingal's bruising grip. Reaching out, Muin took hold of the man's wrist, his fingers tightening until he heard the bones creak.

With a curse, Fingal released Ailene's arm and staggered to his feet. Bent over as he recovered from the blow to his groin, he wheezed. "Stay out of this, Eagle. This is between me and my woman."

"I'm not *your* woman," Ailene hissed. Her face had gone pale, her blue eyes narrowed into glittering slits. She drew the boning knife from her belt and took a step toward him. "Touch me again, and I'll geld you."

"Ailene." Muin cast her a warning look as he stepped in between the two of them. He admired her fire, but even recovering from a well-aimed knee to his cods, Fingal was dangerous.

The Wolf warrior's expression darkened further as his gaze raked Muin from head to foot. "So that's how things are?" he sneered. "You prefer being ridden by a chieftain's son, do you?"

Ailene stepped around Muin, her tall frame bristling with outrage. She held the boning knife with vicious intent, her fingers flexing around its hilt. "Say that twice, and I'll cut your tongue out."

Fingal's lip curled. "Slut. I wager you've been spreading your thighs for half the men in this village ... just not for me. Not anymore."

With a snarl, Ailene leaped for him.

Muin caught her around the waist and pulled her back, shoving her behind him, just as Fingal barreled into him. A heavy fist pummeled into Muin's belly, driving the breath out of him.

Recovering swiftly, Muin shoved the man away, balled his right fist, and slammed it hard into Fingal's nose.

The crunch of breaking sinew and bone followed.

Fingal sank to his knees with an explosive curse, hands going up to where blood gushed from his crushed, bleeding nose.

Muin shook out his hand, stepped back, grabbed Ailene by the arm, and steered her out of the gathering space. The crowd closed behind them, and Fingal's muffled threats faded, replaced by the lilting sound of Eithni's harp and Tea's soulful voice. Most of the gathering had not even noticed the fight, it seemed.

Maneuvering Ailene down the network of narrow streets, Muin did not release his grasp on her arm until the seer dug her heels in and twisted away from him. In the narrow alley, illuminated only by a flickering pitch torch at one end, she turned to him, eyes blazing.

"Let go of me!" she panted. "You shouldn't have interfered."

Surprised by her vehemence, Muin stepped back. "Could you have held your own against Fingal?" he asked.

"I can defend myself."

"By sinking your knife into his gut? How would that help relations between The Eagle and The Wolf?"

Ailene's lip curled. "Ever the peace-weaver, Muin ... just like your father."

Muin went still. "I'm not like him."

"Even so, that wasn't your battle."

"He was pushing himself on you, frightening you." Muin clenched his hands by his sides as he spoke. He could not believe Ailene was speaking to him like this. They had always been kind with each other, and yet the woman before him was a shrill, angry stranger.

A wildly beautiful one.

Under usual circumstances, Ailene possessed a gentle, earthy beauty, but when riled she transformed into the most stunning creature he had ever seen. She stood tall and straight, barely having to lift her chin to meet his eye. Anger made her features more chiseled, darkened her eyes. Her full breasts heaved with the force of the outrage that churned within her.

"Fingal thinks that just because he lies with a woman, it means he has claimed her," Ailene replied, her voice rough. "A confrontation was brewing between us ... but you butting in just made things worse. You should have let me be."

Muin drew in a sharp breath, his own anger kindling. He moved toward Ailene then, forcing her to take a step back against the stacked stone wall of the dwelling behind her. "I couldn't let you be," he growled, his gaze never leaving hers. "And if I ever see you threatened again, I will step in."

Ailene raised her chin a little higher, although a muscle flexed in her jaw, betraying her nervousness. "What if I don't want you to?"

"That doesn't matter. Until the last day I draw breath, I will protect you, Ally. Only The Reaper will stop me."

Ailene's lips parted. "Don't say that," she whispered.

Muin moved closer still. He knew he should not—but he did it anyway. After the argument with his father and the altercation with Fingal, his blood was up; wildness surged through him. "It's the truth."

"You need to let this go." The words were barely audible. "You must."

"I can't."

A heartbeat later he was kissing her.

Muin was not sure how it started. He did not know what madness possessed him to step forward, so that their bodies grazed each other, and to claim her mouth. All he knew was that those full pouty lips had been tempting him from the moment she had rounded on him in the alleyway. He could not blame drink, for he had barely touched any mead during the gathering. He could not blame Ailene for encouraging him either—for she had done the opposite.

And yet there he was, ravaging her mouth like a starved man.

Ailene had gone still against him, her body rigid with shock. Heedless, Muin moved closer still so that he pressed her up against the wall, his hands cupping her face as he deepened the kiss, his tongue parting her lips. She smelled and tasted wonderful: warm and sweet. Better than the scent of heather in bloom in early summer; sweeter than the first gulp of ale after a hard day's work.

Ailene gasped, and he gently bit her full lower lip.

He realized then that something was pressing against his chest. Pulling away, he glanced down to see that her balled fists shoved against him, trying to push him away from her.

Ice washed over Muin like a dip in a wintry loch.

What in the name of the Gods was he doing? What madness had seized him to kiss a woman who had made it clear she did not want him?

Releasing Ailene abruptly, he stepped back. Cold air rushed in between them, and Ailene shivered, pulling the woolen cloak she wore tightly about her.

"I shouldn't have done that." The sound of his voice made him cringe inwardly; it sounded so raw, so desperate. "I'm sorry."

Ailene did not reply. She only stared at him as if he had just sprouted two heads. Her eyes had grown huge upon her pale face. She looked afraid, as if she feared he would maul her again.

Muin moved back from Ailene. "I don't know what came over me," he said. The Reaper take him, how he hated the need, the self-loathing in his voice. "It won't happen again."

And with that, he turned on his heel and strode away.

Ailene leaned back against the wall and tried to quell the rapid beating of her heart. Her legs trembled under her, and she pressed her fisted hands to her thighs, willing her breathing to return to normal.

Watching Muin disappear into the shadows, she slowly raised a hand and touched her lips.

They still burned from his kiss.

He had taken her by complete surprise. One moment they had been arguing, the next his mouth had slanted over hers. And when it did, Ailene ceased to think. The contained power of his body pressed against hers, the hunger yet tenderness in the way his mouth had teased her lips, had driven everything from her mind. And when his tongue had sought entrance to her mouth, her lower belly had caught aflame.

Yet she'd had the presence of mind to try and stop him. Pummeling against the wall of Muin's chest had been like trying to shove a broch aside. But he had realized that she was trying to push him away and had ended the kiss.

And to her eternal shame, loss had arrowed through her when he stepped away.

The horror on Muin's face had cut her deep, as did the pain in his eyes.

She had wanted to tell him all was well, that she was not angry or afraid, just surprised, but her tongue had refused to obey her. She had been unable to do anything save stare at him like a lackwit, while he turned and walked away.

Whispering an oath, Ailene ran a hand over her face.

What had just happened?

She and Muin had quarreled—something they had rarely ever done before the past few days—and then he had embraced her. Although Ailene had only ever lain with Fingal, she had been kissed by a handful of men over the years; usually warriors well into their cups who stole a kiss during one of the many festivals that broke up the year. But none had been like the one Muin had given her.

Muin's kiss was hungry, demanding, and masterful—and it had consumed her, awoken her in ways she found both arousing and disturbing. The sensitive skin between her thighs now ached, and heat pulsed from her lower belly. Her breasts felt swollen and her skin overly sensitive.

Ailene pushed herself up off the wall with a curse this time. This was not what she needed. Her life was already far too complicated, but now things had just escalated to another level.

How would she ever be able to meet Muin's eye again? She did not want him, did not want anyone—and yet her body had just responded to her oldest friend like dry tinder to a flame.

Chapter Fourteen

Think Like Your Enemy

Dun Ringill
Territory of The Serpent

"THE ONLY WAY to win against your enemy is to think like him."

Tormud mac Alec's gravelly voice echoed through the broch, causing all seated at the long table to turn to him.

Cathal glanced up from where he had been toying with his bowl of stew. His appetite was poor these days—it had been ever since Dunchadh's death. Tormud sat a few feet down the table. He was a stocky man who was a couple of years older than Cathal. Heavy-set with penetrating, dark eyes, Tormud's short dark hair was now peppered with grey. A faded blue tattoo marked his right bicep, the mark of The Boar. Even decades living amongst The Serpent could not erase this warrior's origins.

"Is that so," Cathal rumbled, pushing aside his stew. "And how does our enemy think?"

Tormud gave a tight smile. It was rare to see the man show amusement; he was difficult to read at the best of times. "Like me."

Beside Cathal, his son Tamhas snorted. Next to him, Cathal's brother, Artair, smirked.

Of course, Tormud was one of The Boar. He had fought at the Great Wall to the south over twenty years earlier, and instead of returning home to The Winged Isle had gone to live with the Cruthini. He had wed one of Cathal's tribe, a fire-haired wench who had died giving birth to their first child. Cathal had expected The Boar to return to his own people after that, yet he never had.

Instead, he had remained with The Serpent, and when feuding with their neighbors escalated, it had been Tormud's idea to seek a new life for their people upon this isle.

"So, if you had barricaded yourself inside Balintur, what would your next move be?" Cathal asked, ignoring his son's dismissiveness. Tall, broad, and ruddy-haired, Tamhas was a constant reminder of his elder brother, Dunchadh. Tamhas was a good fighter, but he was not half the man Dunchadh had been. Cathal's first-born had been a natural leader: strong and charismatic, the perfect choice to lead this tribe to greatness once Cathal's time passed.

Now that responsibility would fall to Tamhas.

Cathal ground his teeth at the thought.

Tormud poured himself another cup of ale. "First, I would build up my strength again, bring in warriors from the extremities of this isle."

"How many more warriors can they muster?" Mor spoke up then.

Mor, Cathal's only daughter, was seated at the end of the long table. Long dark auburn hair tumbled down her back. She sat up straight and proud as she fixed Tormud with a cool stare Cathal knew well. She might have shared his moss-green eyes, but sometimes her expressions reminded him so much of Lena that it hurt to breathe.

Tormud shifted his dark gaze to Mor. He gave her a long intense look that made Cathal's hackles rise slightly. The Boar had been valuable to him on this campaign, even if Cathal did not always take his advice, but there were times when The Serpent chieftain caught Tormud watching his daughter with hungry eyes.

Cathal did not like it.

Mor isn't for the likes of you.

When his warrior daughter wed, it would not be to a man old enough to be her father. Once he had consolidated his position here, Cathal hoped to find a match for Mor amongst the people of this isle, a chieftain's son perhaps. It would be a handfasting that would win The Serpent much needed allies.

"Dun Ardtreck and Dun Grianan are large strongholds," Tormud replied after a lengthy pause, "but there are also numerous smaller settlements in the north … I believe they could gather another two to three-hundred warriors."

"Wouldn't that empty out their territory?" Mor asked with a frown. "It would leave The Wolf and Stag vulnerable to attack."

A slow smile stretched Cathal's mouth. Like Dunchadh, Mor had a clever, tactical mind. She often offered good advice before battle—unlike her younger brother, Tamhas, who said little during these discussions. Tamhas was frowning now, his gaze riveted upon Cathal.

No love lost there.

"Aye." Tormud's mouth lifted at the corners in another rare smile. "It would."

"And if you were Galan of The Eagle," Cathal spoke up once more, "what would you do once you'd rallied more warriors? Would you attack Dun Ringill?"

The words of Old Murdina came back to Cathal then, and it suddenly felt as if a spider had just crawled down his spine.

The balance of power is shifting.

Tormud sat back, stroking his chin. "Not right away," he replied. "He knows our numbers are strong and that the fort is well-defended. He also realizes that the bitter season is upon us now, and soon the snows will come. To lay siege to Dun Ringill could end up a lengthy campaign, one that might last many moons."

"They could take back An Teanga instead," Tamhas spoke up.

Silence fell at the table. Around them the rumble of conversation at the long tables beneath the chieftain's platform echoed through the broch of Dun Ringill. The aroma of boar stew and peat smoke lay heavy in the air, causing a fug to hover just below the heavy smoke-blackened beams.

Cathal had only lived in this broch three moons, and already it felt like home. He never wanted to leave it. He *never* would leave it.

"An Teanga?" Tormud's heavy-featured face twisted at the suggestion. "Varar mac Urcal would never be able to convince the other chieftains to agree to that."

Tamhas leaned across the table, his gaze spearing Tormud's. "Why not?

"The Boar are loners," the older warrior replied, his dark brows knitting together. "They have never been friends with the other tribes of this isle."

"And yet they joined them to fight against us?" Artair pointed out.

"Only because they had no other choice."

"An Teanga isn't as heavily defended as Dun Ringill," Tamhas countered, stubbornness settling in now. Cathal watched him, surprised. It was rare for the lad to speak so boldly on matters of war. Until now, he had always let Dunchadh and Mor lead discussions. "You said to think like the enemy ... if it was up to me, I'd attack An Teanga."

Tormud barked a laugh. "Then thank the Gods then that you're not in charge, lad."

The rest of the table erupted in laughter. Even Cathal raised a broad smile.

Only Mor and Artair did not join in the mirth. Instead, his brother wore a pensive expression while his daughter's brow furrowed as she watched Tormud. Once the laughter had died down, she shifted her attention to Cathal.

"What of what Old Murdina told you, Da?" she asked. "She said conflict would come before Mid-Winter Fire ... that's just over a moon away."

Cathal nodded and turned his attention back to The Boar. "What of that prediction, Tormud?"

The warrior huffed out a breath and raised his cup of ale to his lips, taking a deep draft. Lowering it, he wiped his mouth with a meaty forearm before replying. "I believe that the united tribes won't attack before spring ... but that doesn't mean we can't lay siege to them. The chieftains of this isle are aggressive, bold. None of them likes being on the defensive. That's why we need to move first."

Cathal listened to Tormud, his smile widening further. The Boar was cunning. Not for the first time, Cathal was pleased he had listened to Tormud's council in the past. The man had not steered him wrong thus far. He had only seen defeat when he had disregarded the warrior's advice. "So, we should hit Balintur?"

Tormud grunted. "Aye."

"And why would we hit them where they are at their strongest?"

Tormud grinned, showing his teeth. "We too are strong, Cathal. Balintur is the keystone in the arch ... if it falls, this isle is yours."

Cathal picked up his own cup and drank deeply, draining it. Both his son and Tormud had given him ideas to mull over. "Further protect An Teanga or attack Balintur?" he rumbled. "I will think on this."

Murmuring went up amongst his warriors, rippling down the table. Those at the tables below stopped eating and drinking and turned their gazes to the platform at the far end of the feasting hall. They were curious to know what had been discussed here, but they would learn of it soon enough.

Cathal sat back in his chair. It was a heavy seat, with carven eagle wings decorating the back. This summer he would have another chair made, one that would have serpents wreathing the armrests. However, he would keep this chair in his alcove, as a trophy.

His gaze slid down the table, taking in the eager faces of the men and women seated there.

Everyone seemed animated, excited about what the future held—everyone except Mor and Tamhas. Mor's expression was blank, her moss-green eyes shuttered as she sipped at her ale. Tamhas on the other hand was frowning, and the knuckles of his hand that gripped his cup were white. He was staring at Tormud with a look of simmering dislike.

The bandruí's warning nagged at Cathal then.

Someone will betray you.

When he had returned from visiting Old Murdina, Cathal had informed his warriors about her predictions regarding future conflict with the folk of this isle. But he had kept her warning of betrayal to himself. Instead, he decided to keep a close eye on those of his inner circle. If someone was sharpening their knife against him, he would ferret them out.

Yet, a few days had passed since he had visited the seer, and Cathal still did not have any idea who the traitor might be.

His most trusted warriors had fought at his side through many campaigns. Some had saved his life during battles. Others, like Tormud, had sacrificed much to follow Cathal.

That left Cathal's own kin.

Mor was trustworthy. The lass had a quiet, introspective nature that made her hard to read at times, yet her loyalty was unquestionable. Artair had always followed him without question; his younger brother had never sought to challenge his authority over the tribe.

That only left Tamhas.

He could not imagine his son betraying him—but the look in the young man's green eyes told another story. Tamhas resented Tormud. He did not like the influence the warrior had.

Tamhas had long dwelt in Dunchadh's shadow, and he was eager to prove himself now that his elder brother was dead.

Cathal's gaze narrowed as he continued to observe his son. He remembered his grandfather telling him once that the worst betrayals often occurred between family members.

I must watch him.

Chapter Fifteen

Turning Away

Balintur
Territory of The Eagle

MUIN SLID THE blade along the whet-stone in long, even strokes. He sat alone in the small dwelling he shared with Talor. The door was open, and the watery dawn light filtered in, bringing with it the aroma of oatcakes fresh off the griddle and the murmur of voices of folk getting ready for departure.

Ignoring it all, Muin continued to sharpen the blade. The action steadied him; it was his ritual before going into battle. Sharpening his blade focused his thoughts, drove out distractions.

It was a fine sword, molded in the style of the Caesars. His uncle Tarl had brought back weapons from the Great Wall to the south, daggers and swords among them. Muin's sword had a wide cast iron blade with a rounded tip. The blade had a bronze pommel and an ivory handle. His father had gifted it to Muin on his thirteenth birthday.

At the thought of Galan, Muin's jaw clenched.

He was still sore after their argument the evening before—although another incident had darkened his mood further.

That kiss.

He had made a few mistakes in his life, including telling Ailene how he felt about her. But none had been as foolish as kissing her.

The look on her face when he stepped away had been like a punch to guts.

"Are you ready, cousin?" Talor stuck his head in through the door. The warrior's face was tense, his tone clipped. "The army is going to move out soon."

"Aye." Muin rose to his feet and sheathed the blade over his shoulder with one easy movement. Then, picking up a light leather pack, he followed Talor out into the grey morning.

A drizzle fell, shrouding the surrounding landscape in tones of milky white and grey. It was poor weather for traveling, although the cloud cover would make it easier for them to move unseen.

The plan was to cut east from Balintur, journeying deep into the mountainous heart of the isle, before traveling down the east coast and approaching An Teanga from the north-east. It was quite a loop, and many furlongs longer than if they had entered Boar territory directly. Yet it meant that the enemy would be far less likely to spot them.

Striding through the village, Muin focused his thoughts on what was to come. It was easier to think about the upcoming battle than on what he was leaving behind. It was truly over between him and Ailene now. In just a few days, the friendship he had believed would endure a lifetime had disintegrated completely.

A dull ache had taken up residence deep within Muin's chest, twisting whenever his thoughts shifted to Ailene.

Then don't think about her, he counseled himself, irritation arrowing through him.

Around them an expectant, tense air had settled over the village—like an indrawn breath. Many of the faces they passed, most of them folk staying behind, were somber, their gazes shuttered. Bairns clung to their mother's skirts, watching wide-eyed as heavily-armed warriors strode past. Just like between the chieftains, feelings toward this campaign were divided among the united tribes. More than a few had misgivings. Even so, the chieftains had made their decision.

The army was moving out, and An Teanga was its destination.

"You're quiet this morning," Talor observed, falling into step beside his cousin.

Muin cast him a shuttered look. "You know I'm not one to fill silences."

Talor huffed a laugh, although his gaze remained upon Muin's face. "Aye ... but you have a scowl to make even your friends keep their distance."

Muin shrugged off the comment.

Talor shot him a shrewd look. "I saw Fingal mac Diarmid after you broke his nose. He's swearing vengeance."

Muin snorted. "Let him."

Talor continued to observe Muin with an intensity that made him stiffen. He knew that look. His cousin was about to start prying. "I take it things haven't progressed with Ailene?" he asked quietly.

Muin clenched his jaw. "No."

"Maybe you need to try harder. You could always—"

"Enough," Muin growled. "Leave it, Talor."

His cousin's brow furrowed, but this time he held his tongue.

The pair entered the clearing at the heart of the village, where a dense crowd of warriors waited. A low rumble of conversation lifted into the mist. The men and women spoke amongst themselves in low, determined voices. Muin could not help but notice that the different tribes grouped together.

Despite that they were all fighting on the same side these days, the old divisions still remained. Muin was no different, for he headed toward where a large company of Eagle warriors had gathered.

Everyone was dressed and armed for battle. Some men went scantily clad, while others like Muin, wore plaid breeches and leather vests. Many of the women, Fina included, had donned little more than two bands of leather, covering their loins and breasts. Warriors had painted swirls of blue woad on their faces and exposed limbs. Sharpened iron gleamed despite the dull dawn: spears, axes, swords, and pikes.

Still frowning after Muin's biting reply, Talor ran an eye over him. "Is that all you're carrying into battle?"

Muin shrugged. He wore his sword on his back and a dagger strapped to his right thigh. "It's all I need."

As he was staying behind, Talor was unarmed this morning. However, Muin knew that his cousin never went into battle without an arsenal of weaponry: a bow and a quiver of arrows, two axes on his back, and a collection of knives strapped all over his body.

Fina strode over to them then, a quiver of arrows over one shoulder and a sword swinging at her side. She had painted whorls and designs in blue over her bare arms and legs.

"We're going soon," she informed them, her expression as fierce as her appearance. "Ailene just has to perform blessings first."

Muin went still at the mention of the bandruí. He had hoped to leave without seeing her.

And yet there she was, walking barefoot through the crowd, a clay pot full of burning dried herbs in one hand, a divining wand in the other.

Deep in concentration, Ailene had not seen him. She looked different this morning; her hair was braided and pulled up to coil around the crown of her head. She wore bracelets and necklaces that rattled as she walked. Thin streaks of woad decorated her cheeks.

She did not look like the lass he had grown up with; Ailene appeared older, more distant.

Folk nodded and murmured to her when she passed, while Ailene blessed them with her wand. The smell of incense drifted over Muin as she approached.

Panic surged within him. He could not face her, not after last night.

Clenching his fists at his sides, he turned away, and remained that way until Ailene had passed by.

"What's wrong with you this morning?" Fina's sharp voice roused Muin from his brooding.

He turned to find his cousin scowling at him. Muin frowned in response. "Excuse me?"

"Ailene just tried to bless you, and you gave her your back."

"I don't need a blessing."

Fina's gaze narrowed. "Of course you do. Have you and Ailene fallen out?"

Muin heaved in a deep breath. He had almost reached the limit of his patience. First Talor and now Fina—he was tired of their meddling. Could they not leave him alone? He had bitten Talor's head off earlier, but Fina was not the sort to leave well alone.

He decided that ignoring her was the best option. Without answering, Muin simply walked off, leaving Fina glaring at his back.

Ailene glanced over her shoulder, at where Muin was now moving away from the company of Eagle warriors. He shouldered his way through the crowd, his broad back rigid. Fina watched him go, her expression thunderous.

Humiliation pulsed hot through Ailene. *Rude bastard.* She could not believe he had just shunned her.

In front of everyone.

Choking back the outrage that made her hands tremble, Ailene forced herself to focus on the task at hand.

She whispered a blessing and dipped her wand over the shoulders of the two chieftains who would lead the mission to An Teanga: Varar and Galan. The chieftains of The Stag and The Wolf would remain behind to protect Balintur. However, they were sending warriors on the campaign. Wid's only surviving son, Calum, led The Wolf, and Tadhg's eldest daughter, Moira, led The Stag.

Ailene moved over to Calum and Moira, holding the cresset of burning herbs aloft so that they could inhale it.

"May The Warrior guide your blades," she murmured, her voice husky with the embarrassment that still burned bright within her. "May The Hag protect you." Moira, a dark-haired, statuesque young woman, favored her with a tense smile. Calum, a stocky young man with a short beard, nodded his thanks.

Unlike Muin, neither of them turned their back on her.

Ailene's temper flared once more. To think that she had actually felt sorry for him last night, had keenly felt his mortification. She had lain awake during the night, wondering if she should go to him so that they could at least part on good terms.

He had not even wanted to bid her farewell.

Her cheeks still glowed with embarrassment. She had seen the shock on the warriors' faces surrounding them when Muin had given her his back. Fina had looked as if she wanted to launch herself at her cousin and hit him around the head.

Enough ... don't waste your thoughts on him.

Ailene focused her attention instead on the surrounding crowd. She sensed the nervous energy of the amassed companies of warriors around her, their eagerness to move out. Many of them shifted restlessly, while others began to beat their weapons against their oaken shields as they awaited the horn that would signal their departure.

Stepping back, Ailene whispered one final incantation and glanced over at where Galan and Varar still watched her intently. "It is done," she announced. "The Gods will be with you."

"Can I speak to you for a moment?"

Eithni glanced up from where she was adding salt to her turnip and cabbage pottage. "Of course ... take a seat."

Ailene entered the round-house and moved to the hearth, lowering herself onto a stool. She suddenly felt foolish for rushing here as soon as the army had departed. But the moment the warriors had gone, emptying Balintur, she had been anxious and on-edge. She needed to confide in someone, or she would burst.

"I have a problem ... and I don't know how to resolve it."

Eithni brushed the salt off her hands, alarm flashing across her fine features. "What is it, lass?"

"It's Muin," Ailene replied, before drawing in a deep breath and exhaling slowly. "He's in love with me."

The healer stiffened, her eyes widening. "He told you this?"

"Aye ... a few days ago."

Eithni reached for a damp cloth and wiped her hands. "You don't share his feelings, I take it?"

Ailene dug her fingernails into her palms so hard that she winced. "No ... but things have gotten ... complicated."

Eithni crossed to the stool next to Ailene and lowered herself onto it. The pair of them were alone in the round-house. Eara had gone off to collect water, Bonnie was at sword practice, and Donnel was taking a shift guarding the wall. "Start at the beginning," she said gently. "I'm listening."

Ailene ran a hand over her face. She did not really want to face all of this, and yet she longed to unburden herself, to reveal the truth to one person at least.

Slowly, she began to speak. She told the tale from the beginning, from the evening of the council when they had decided to send a scouting party to An Teanga, to the events of the night before.

She left nothing out.

By the time she halted, her face was burning like an ember and sweat was trickling between her shoulder blades and breasts.

Eithni was watching her with a soft expression that made Ailene's belly contract. Silence stretched between them for a few moments, before the healer reached out and took Ailene's hand. "Are you sure you don't have feelings for Muin?"

Ailene swallowed hard. "Of course I do ... I love him ... as a friend. He's always been part of my life."

"I wasn't talking about friendship, lass."

Ailene stared back at her. "I don't know," she whispered, "I really don't. He's made me so angry of late. When he turned his back on me earlier, I wanted to slap him."

Eithni sighed, her slender fingers gently squeezing Ailene's hand. "Letting someone into your heart can be frightening," she murmured, "especially if you've been hurt."

Eithni's eyes shadowed then. Ailene knew of the healer's history. Before falling in love with Donnel, she had sworn to spend her life alone after being brutalized by a Wolf warrior who had murdered her brother and taken control of The Wolf stronghold, Dun Ardtreck. It had taken a lot for Eithni to trust again—but in the end Donnel's love had won her over.

But Ailene had never been harshly treated. She had no reason to keep Muin at arm's length. She did not understand this wall that she had built around her, or how to tear it down. She was not sure she wanted to; there was safety in walling yourself off from others.

"Maybe seers are meant to live alone," Ailene said finally. "Ruith never took a husband."

Eithni inclined her head. "She had her reasons ... did Ruith ever speak to you of her past?"

Ailene shook her head. "I only know she also lost her parents young."

"Aye ... but not like you did. Her father killed her mother in a jealous rage when Ruith was only five. The folk of Dun Ringill cast him out in punishment, to die alone. Ruith told me the story once, many years ago, at a gathering of the tribes. She admitted to me that she had never gotten over what happened, or trusted a man ever since." Eithni broke off there, her gaze scanning Ailene's face. "Ruith remained alone out of fear of being hurt, not because she was happier that way."

Ailene stared back at her, surprise filtering through her. She had lived with Ruith for years, and not once had the old woman ever told her that story. She wished Ruith had confided in her.

"You took your parents deaths hard," Eithni said after a pause. "I was worried about you after we lost Mael."

When Ailene did not reply, a smile curved Eithni's mouth. "Not everyone we love abandons us," she said, squeezing Ailene's hand once more. "Happiness is hard to achieve if we push others away. We have to risk our hearts if we want to live a full life."

Chapter Sixteen

A Chill Premonition

TIREDNESS PRESSED DOWN on Ailene as she readied herself to retire to her furs for the night. She moved around her hut, going through her usual tasks. Now that the evenings were getting cold, she made sure the hearth had a fresh lump of peat upon it. She also put out a clean wooden cup on her work table and the ingredients for her morning oatcakes. Ailene liked to be organized in the mornings.

The routine soothed her, distracted her from her churning thoughts. She had been in a state all day, unable to focus on her usual chores.

Going to see Eithni had not been a good idea. Instead of calming her, the healer had merely made Ailene even more confused. She had suggested that Ailene's feelings for Muin ran deeper than she realized, that her anger toward him masked another emotion—one she did not want to face.

"Enough," Ailene muttered, scrubbing her hand over her face. "No more thinking tonight ... no more worrying."

Undressing quickly, for despite the glowing fire pit, the evening was nippy, she climbed naked into her nest of furs. She then pulled them up under her chin.

Ailene lay there, staring up at the rafters, and wondered if she would manage to get any sleep at all. Despite that her body and mind cried out for rest, her thoughts still whirled. Eithni's well-meaning advice plagued her.

We have to risk our hearts if we want to live a full life.

Is that what she was doing ... hiding from life? Ailene's head ached; she was tired of going over and over this, like a rat chasing its tail. She wanted oblivion to chase away her worries.

She had thought sleep would elude her, however, the warmth and softness of the furs cocooned her, and in the end, fatigue won, pulling her down into its clutches. Ailene fell into a deep slumber.

She dreamed of water.

It slid over her limbs, bone-numbingly cold yet as gentle as a mother's touch. Ailene swam swiftly through the darkness, diving through the water like a selkie, her long hair trailing behind her.

Surfacing, she inhaled the crisp, smoke-laced night air, her gaze traveling north.

A great stone broch rose against the horizon, its squat, dark outline silhouetted against the star-sprinkled sky. Treading water, Ailene tried to get her bearings. The broch was familiar, although she could not quite place it.

The tower sat at the end of a promontory, the low outline of hills behind it. A row of braziers encircled its base, throwing out golden light over the surrounding loch. It was not Dun Ringill, for her home perched upon a cliff and was surrounded by a high wall.

Recognition flooded over Ailene then, memories of a past gathering of the tribes.

An Teanga.

As Ailene floated there, she saw shapes move past her. It was a moonless night, which made the stars shine even brighter. Warriors swam by, heading toward the stony shore that surrounded the base of the broch.

Ailene did not follow them. Instead, she continued to tread water, watching as figures climbed out of the water and crept around the edge of the tower. They were heading toward its only entrance, which was east-facing.

Surprise feathered across Ailene. During their scouting mission, Fina had reported that there had been warriors stationed around the base of the broch. Yet tonight it appeared undefended.

The warriors of the united tribes continued to climb out of the water, moving up the bank to where braziers burned. But they had not gone more than a few yards when a tide of warriors, blades glinting in the starlight, flowed out from the shadows.

Ailene's breathing hitched.

The Serpent had lain in wait, preferring to watch the approach across the loch from the shadows so that any enemy would think the shore was undefended.

Ailene opened her mouth to shout a warning to the others still swimming past her. However, no sound escaped her lips. She was struck mute.

At least two dozen attackers had reached the rocks now. They clambered up only to find themselves beset upon.

Panic exploded within Ailene. She had to warn them—she had to do something.

Striking out, she swam in long strokes toward the shore. The cold bit at her skin, turning her feet and hands numb, yet she paid it no mind.

She crawled out of the water and discovered that she was naked.

Surprised, Ailene ran her hands down her wet flanks. What was she doing out here anyway? She had never been a strong swimmer.

Craning her neck, she fixed her attention on the figures a few yards above her. Iron glinted in the light of the braziers; the fires illuminated the grim faces of the men and women who now fought to the death.

And in amongst them, Ailene spied a familiar figure.

Big and broad-shouldered, Muin was hard to miss. Ailene had watched him at sword-play in the warriors' enclosure enough times to recognize his fighting style immediately as well. He fought boldly, using his blade to slash and stab with ruthless efficiency.

Muin fought savagely now, and there was an edge of desperation to it. Ailene realized, with rising panic, that he was surrounded and outnumbered. Despite his strength, Muin was struggling to hold them all off.

And as she looked on, unable to help or to warn him, a huge man with wild hair that shone red-gold in the brazier light lunged at him, axe aloft.

The axe blade slammed into Muin's neck, and he went down.

Ice washed over Ailene. She opened her mouth in a silent scream, while around her, everything went black.

Trembling, she blinked—and when she opened her eyes again, she was no longer standing naked on the edge of a loch, but instead in the midst of swirling mist, before a line of cairns.

A crow's caw echoed through the damp air, and then Ailene caught the sound of a woman singing a lament for the dead. The singer's voice trembled as grief threatened to overwhelm her.

Ailene did not want to move, and yet her feet refused to obey her. She was dressed now in a long tunic, with a fur mantle around her shoulders, as she walked barefoot across the frozen ground.

The mist cleared, and a crowd of mourners appeared before a burial mound. Heads bowed in grief, the sounds of gentle sobbing drifted across to Ailene, mingling with the sad lament.

Tea stood at the edge of the mourners, head held high as she sang. Tears ran down her proud face, even as her voice shook.

Ailene walked closer, dread mounting with each step.

There, upon a litter lay Muin mac Galan. Dressed in black leather, his strong hands clasped over the hilt of his sword, his handsome face did not look serene in repose. His expression was stern, his skin unnaturally pale.

A sob rose in Ailene's chest, the crushing pain almost unbearable.

"Muin ... no!"

Ailene sat up, heart slamming against her ribs.

Gods, not again.

Darkness shrouded her, save for the welcoming glow of embers in the nearby fire pit. Like the last dream, in which she had first witnessed Muin's burial, Ailene found herself sweat-soaked and shaking in the aftermath.

But this dream had been far more detailed than the first, far more vivid.

She had been there, had felt the cold water brush against her skin and the frozen ground numbing her bare feet.

Trembling, Ailene gathered a fur around her nakedness and got up, shuffling over to the fire pit.

Seated there, she cupped her face in her hands.

The Reaper take me, I have seen the future.

She had been so relieved when Muin had returned from the scouting mission. Afterward, she had cast off her dream as folly. Yet the vision she had just experienced could not be ignored. Her dream had not warned her of that scouting mission to An Teanga, but of the siege itself.

The journey that Muin had just departed for.

He had not even let her bless him before leaving.

She had seen it all, seen him cut down by a mortal wound to the neck. Muin would not survive this campaign, would not return to Balintur.

Panic surged within Ailene. Heart pounding, she lurched to her feet, clutching the fur around her.

Muin could not die. She would not let him. Sweat beaded across her skin once more, as a sickening realization settled over her.

Life was not worth living without Muin mac Galan.

"Gods," she whispered. Bile rose up, stinging the back of Ailene's throat. "Eithni was right."

She could not bear facing the future without him. Ailene's vision blurred, but as she faced the truth about her feelings toward her oldest friend, guilt surged within her.

She had dismissed that earlier dream, when she should have heeded its warning. Muin should not have gone with the others. If she had warned Galan, he would have forbidden it.

Ailene started to shuffle back and forth across the dirt floor of her hut, agitated now. She had to do something, yet panic had momentarily rendered her witless.

"I have to tell someone," she muttered.

Initially, all she had been able to think about was Muin. But it was not just his life at risk. Her vision of An Teanga had given her a chill premonition of what was to come. The warriors of the united tribes would swim in from the loch to a slaughter. Someone needed to reach the army and warn them.

She had to let Tadhg mac Fortrenn and Wid mac Manus know.

Ailene shrugged off the fur and reached for her clothing. It was a chill night so she pulled on a thin linen tunic, a heavy plaid skirt, a long-sleeved woolen tunic, and a leather vest that she laced at the front. Then she hauled on fur-lined boots and a fur cloak.

Moving toward the door, Ailene's step suddenly faltered.

There was no time to go to the chieftains, no time to convince them of what she had seen. If she rode after the army now, she could be well away from Balintur before the first blush of dawn stained the eastern sky.

She could not remain in Balintur while Muin edged toward his doom. She did not want to be forced to wait here, anxious to know whether the slaughter had taken place. She had to warn Muin—she had to warn all of them.

This was her mess, and she would be the one to fix it.

Grabbing a leather satchel, Ailene stuffed a wedge of cheese, left-over oatcakes, and a bladder of water inside. Then she strapped her only weapon, her father's slender boning knife, around her waist.

Pulling up the hood of her fur cloak, Ailene made for the door.

She was ready to go.

The guards at the gate looked surprised to see a woman astride a shaggy dun pony appear out of the darkness.

One of the men stepped forward, peering up at her.

"Ailene, is that you?" He was an Eagle warrior, a handful of years older than Ailene.

"Aye, Macum," she greeted the man with a brittle smile, pushing back her hood slightly so he could see her face. "Good morning."

The warrior raised a dark eyebrow. "A bit early for a ride, isn't it?"

"I need to gather herbs," she replied, keeping the smile plastered to her face. "Ones vital to weaving protection charms around this village."

"You have to depart now?"

"Aye ... there is a special variety of moss that grows in the foot hills of the Black Cuillins. If I depart early, I can be there and back in a day."

"We should send an escort with you."

Ailene frowned. The Hag curse him, she wished another had been posted at the gates; Macum, whose wife had just given birth to their fourth daughter, was known for being overly protective with women.

"Stop your fussing," she said, waving him off. "I'm riding north into safe lands. I don't need an escort."

Macum looked unconvinced. "It's cold out, and there was a moonbow earlier."

Ailene fought the urge to scowl. A moonbow—a pink hue over the moon—was a sign of coming bad weather. She did not relish the idea of riding through the wind and rain to reach the army. But it could not be helped. This had to be done. The only way they would keep her here would be if they tied her up. She would not be kept from Muin's side.

"A little rain doesn't bother me," she replied. Her face was starting to ache from the effort it was taking to keep her smile in place. "The sooner I set off, the sooner I'll be back."

Macum watched her for a moment longer before heaving a long-suffering sigh.

Ailene was fortunate. Few women, beside those who were warriors, were allowed to ride out on their own. But Ailene was not like other females. Macum, like many within these walls, minded her. She was allowed freedom that wives and mothers were not.

"Very well, lass." He stepped back and motioned for the other guards to open the gates. "Watch how you go though."

"I will," Ailene assured him.

Moments later she was riding through the gates into a cold, windy night. It was very late, or early depending on how you saw things, and the moon had set. The fires atop the walls of Balintur illuminated the surrounding hills, and when Ailene glanced up, she could see the starry sky behind racing clouds.

Urging her pony on, her heels sinking into its furry flanks, Ailene rode north. This was not the direction of travel she intended, but she needed to go this way, just in case the guards at the gate were watching her depart.

Once she crested the hill and Balintur was no longer visible at her back, she reined the pony east and circled around.

The pony belonged to her. His name was Eòrna—Barley. Named so, for during the summer, the gelding's coat looked like sun-ripened grain. This time of year, however, when he grew his thick winter coat, his color darkened. Like the other ponies of this isle, Eòrna was heavy-set with a bristling mane, long tail, and large feathered hooves. He had a dogged, calm temperament, and Ailene trusted him completely.

They rode over bare hills, cutting east in the direction the army had taken. Up ahead the outlines of great mountain peaks rose against the star-strewn sky. She would have to traverse those ranges, cutting between them to reach the eastern coast.

A stinging wind gusted against Ailene's cheeks as she urged Eòrna into a choppy trot. In order to ride astride the gelding's barrel-like sides, she had been forced to hike her skirt up, exposing her bare legs to the elements.

A grim smile tugged at Ailene's mouth then. She was no warrior. She had seen how scantily clad Fina had been when she left for battle. It was as if the cold did not touch her. In contrast, Ailene was fully clothed and wore a heavy fur cloak around her shoulders.

She certainly was not at risk of freezing out here, but unlike Fina, she was a woman who preferred the comforts of home to braving the elements.

Ailene's smile faded then. But brave them she would—for Muin.

Chapter Seventeen

Journeying East

AILENE TRAVELED LONG through the darkness, continuing even as the eastern sky grew light and sun kissed the tawny slopes of the mountains that now loomed above her.

Just after dawn, she halted for a short spell, stopping Eòrna by a burn so that the pony could rest and take a drink. She ate a few mouthfuls of oatcake and cheese too, although her appetite was poor this morning. Her belly had tied itself in knots in the aftermath of that dream.

Every time she closed her eyes, she could see Muin falling, an axe-blade buried in the back of his neck.

Nausea crept up her throat once more, panic assailing her in a sickening wave.

The thought of never hearing the low rumble of his voice, never again seeing the gentle curve of his mouth when he smiled, or the warmth in those slate-grey eyes, made it hard to breathe.

Muin had stolen up on her. All these years, she had seen him only as a friend, but now she would never view him that way again.

He was her other half, and if she lost him, it would shatter her—just as her mother had withered and died after losing Ailene's father.

Mounting her pony once more, Ailene pressed on. The mountains rose above her now, massive peaks that dwarfed her. The landscape of the interior of this isle never failed to make her feel tiny and unimportant in the scale of things. These mountains would stand forever, yet her life-span would be over in the blinking of an eye.

The wind howled through the pass, catching at Ailene's cloak. She kept an eye out for signs of the army that had also traveled this way, and soon found them: hoof prints marked the soft earth.

She was headed in the right direction.

Traveling on her own made Ailene nervous. She had spent her life surrounded by the close-knit community at Dun Ringill. Every time she had journeyed farther afield, she always had company. Out here in the wilderness, with only her pony and the odd bird of prey that glided overhead for company, she felt vulnerable. Ailene glanced around as she rode, eyes scanning her surroundings for any sign of danger.

Unconcerned by his rider's nervousness, Eòrna plodded on.

The rain swept in from the east, heavy curtains of it that blanketed the sky and pummeled the ponies, men, and women who made their way through the shallow valley.

Muin bowed his head and rounded his shoulders. The rain had held off for most of the day, but now it drove in: icy, stinging needles that made the ponies hold their heads low and flatten their ears back.

Glancing down, Muin caught sight of the bracelet upon his wrist. The leather was sodden, and the turquoise stones gleamed wetly. The morning they had left Balintur, he had been tempted to tear off Ailene's gift to him—but something prevented him.

Just because she did not want him, did not mean that he could not always keep a piece of her with him. It seemed childish to cast away something that had been made especially for him. The bracelet was a reminder of happier days, of a woman he would never stop loving.

The army of just over two hundred warriors snaked its way toward the eastern coast. Muin knew they were close, and so when the mountains pulled back, and a grey, churning expanse of water appeared on the eastern horizon, he was not surprised. Despite that around half their number marched on foot, the army had made good time inland. They had camped in the midst of the mountains, the sides of their hide tents snapping and billowing in the wind, before setting off again at first light.

This time tomorrow they would reach their destination, just a few furlongs north-east of An Teanga, where they would ready themselves for the siege.

A horn blew then, its mournful wail cutting through the howl of the wind.

Varar and Galan had decided to make camp.

Relieved, for his body ached from being in the saddle for the past two days, Muin dismounted his heavy-set black stallion and led it over to where others were tying their ponies up under a row of birches. The trees had nearly entirely lost their leaves, so they did not provide much shelter. However, it was the best they could manage, and men were already erecting hide awnings between the trees to keep the worst of the rain and wind off the ponies.

Muin's pony, Feannag—Crow—nudged at his master's shoulder as he tied him up. Turning to him, Muin slapped the stallion's muscular neck. "Hungry, lad?"

The pony nudged him once more, this time in the chest.

Smiling, Muin fitted Feannag with a nose bag; the cloth pouch contained a few handfuls of crushed oats and barley. He then took a twist of wet grass and began to rub the pony down.

And all the while, the wind howled like a demon.

Around him Muin heard muffled cursing as warriors struggled to erect their tents in the gale. They put them up amongst the birch thicket, with a wide awning covering a central fire pit.

When Muin finished seeing to his pony, he made his way to the heart of the camp to find that the others had somehow managed to light a fire. It smoked and guttered, yet tender orange flames now licked up into the gloaming.

Muttering, warriors jostled around it, trying to get warm.

"Why does it always rain whenever we go to battle?" Fina appeared at Muin's side, handing him a wedge of stale bread and cheese.

Muin managed a smile. "Aye ... it's almost as if the Gods start fighting amongst themselves when they know blood is about to be shed."

Fina grinned. "Just as long as it's Serpent blood." She glanced up then, at where the sky was now completely obscured by dark cloud. "I can imagine The Warrior up there, beating his battle drum."

Muin observed Fina, noting the gleam in her eye, the eagerness on her face. Fina was a born warrior, although ever since her union with Varar mac Urcal, there was a steadiness to her that had been missing earlier. Before falling in love with Varar, there had been a recklessness, a wildness to his cousin that had often concerned Muin.

She had often teased him when he voiced his concerns. But Muin had no need to look after his fiery cousin now, not when she had Varar at her side.

Meeting Muin's eye, Fina's grin faded. "Talor told me about you and Ailene," she said quietly.

Heat flushed through Muin. "Talor's got a big mouth," he growled. "Remind me to shove his teeth down his throat when we get back to Balintur."

"Don't blame him," Fina replied with a shake of her head. "After you turned your back on Ailene, I knew something was amiss. I bailed Talor up before we left Balintur and made him tell me."

Muin's fingers tightened around the hunk of bread he held. He did not want anyone knowing of his humiliation. It was bad enough that he had confided in Talor. The last thing he needed was both his cousins feeling sorry for him.

"Don't look so angry," Fina chastised him, digging her elbow into Muin's ribs. "I'm not going to tell you what to do or how to behave." She paused there, her grey eyes shadowing. "I'm just sorry ... for I believe you two would be great together."

Muin tore his gaze away to stare at the dancing flames in the fire pit before him. "What makes you think that?"

"You balance each other ... like Varar and I do."

Muin's mouth curved in a humorless smile. "I don't think that comparison works, cousin."

"Aye, it does. You know you've met the right person, for they bring out the best in you, and smooth out the rough edges."

Muin snorted in an attempt to cover up his discomfort. This conversation was starting to make him squirm. Of course, Talor did not know about Muin's last disgrace; after his shame at Gateway, Muin had avoided confiding in his mouthy cousin.

However, Fina was a woman—and hopefully as such had more understanding of the situation. Shifting his attention from the fire, Muin met Fina's gaze once more. "I kissed Ailene."

Fina stared back at him a moment, before she threw her head back and laughed.

Muin stiffened. "This amuses you?"

"The tragic look on your face," Fina gasped, wiping her eyes. "Gods, Muin. You take *everything* so seriously."

Muin muttered a curse and raked a hand through his damp hair. If the rain had not been pelting down, he would have walked off. As it was, there was nowhere to go without getting soaked.

Sensing his darkening mood, Fina sobered. "Well ... how did she react to the kiss?"

Muin scowled back at her. He was not discussing this.

"Did she slap your face?"

"No."

"Did she try to knee you in the cods or start weeping?"

"No," he snapped this time.

"How did she react?"

"She pushed me away."

Fina frowned. "So, you don't think she enjoyed it?"

Muin twisted, giving Fina his profile once more. "No," he ground the word out. "She didn't."

Chapter Eighteen

Taking Shelter

AILENE FOUND A place to take shelter for the night, while a grey dusk settled over the land. Frowning as a particularly vicious squall buffeted pony and rider, she guided Eòrna across the bottom of a shallow valley carpeted on one side by a hazel thicket. As Macum had predicted, the bad weather had arrived.

She was not fond of storms, but at least there was no thunder or lightning with this one, just howling wind and driving rain that chilled her to the marrow. Shivering, Ailene tied Eòrna up to a tree. She made sure to give the pony enough rope so that he could graze a little overnight. Built like a barrel, the gelding was not likely to starve if he did not have a meal of crushed oats and a manger of hay. Even so, Ailene fed him a piece of oatcake, before she settled down for the night.

Ailene peered up at her choice of shelter, her frown deepening. Being deciduous, the hazel tree did not offer much protection from the elements. However, in the wild, open landscape of this part of The Winged Isle, it was the best she could find.

With a grunt, Eòrna lowered his bulk onto the ground next to her. Grateful, Ailene shifted close to his furry back. The pony was an effective shelter against the biting prevailing wind.

Pulling her fur cloak close, Ailene settled against the gelding's warmth. It would be a long, cold night, but since she did not know this area at all, she would not risk traveling in the dark, especially in such foul weather.

Around her the rain still drove in; dark clouds obliterated the sky and the surrounding mountains. It was as if the world had shrunk to this forgotten valley, and this hazel thicket.

Ailene stroked Eòrna's luxurious dun coat as she tried to get comfortable. The action soothed her jangled nerves and eased the worries that had plagued her all day. Even so, one surfaced, gnawing at her.

What if I'm too late?

Icy dread settled in the pit of her belly. Ailene clenched her jaw, pushed the thought aside, and shifted position against the pony. Her thigh muscles were stiffening already, as she was unused to riding long distances. The wind buffeted her, its probing fingers attempting to get through her fur cloak. However, there was not any point in trying to light a fire in this weather. She would just have to brave the cold and try to get some rest.

Stop fretting, she counselled herself as she reached into her satchel for some cheese. *It's not helping.*

Nibbling at her supper, she surveyed the bleak valley where she had stopped for the night. The weather was so foul, and she had been in such a hurry to find shelter, that she had barely taken notice of her surroundings.

As such, she had missed the fairy mound upon the opposite side of the vale. It was around thirty feet distant, a smooth green hillock studded with stones.

Ailene's gaze fixed upon the mound, and she went still, swallowing her mouthful of cheese with difficulty.

It was not wise to make camp near such a place.

Ailene had heard many a tale of unwary travelers or lovers who had fallen asleep too close to the mounds, only to be stolen away by the Aos Sí, or the Fair Folk—the fairy people who dwelt in the forgotten corners of this isle. Beautiful yet dangerous, the Fair Folk were to be avoided unless you came bearing gifts to lay before their homes.

Ruith had taught Ailene charms to protect against the caprices of the Aos Sí, and Ailene murmured one now.

They were known to emerge at dusk, but hopefully, the foul weather would keep them away. Even so, Ailene tensed. She had been so immersed in her worries over Muin, she had not taken proper note of her surroundings.

The daylight continued to fade as sheets of rain swept across the valley. Ailene huddled against her pony. Despite her tension, tiredness washed over her; she had been traveling since before dawn.

She was just starting to feel drowsy, her eyelids slowly closing, when she saw lights appear in the gloaming.

The lights floated toward Ailene like fireflies. Blinking, she tried to focus. Were they torches? Had someone else sought refuge overnight in the valley?

Sucking in a deep breath, she reached for the knife at her waist.

The lights did not belong to the folk of this isle, but to someone else.

Slender figures dressed in long silvery robes emerged from the driving rain. Even from this distance Ailene spied their beauty. Many had yellow or silvery hair and gold-hued skin. Their robes shimmered as if they had been woven with starlight. The rain and wind did not appear to touch them.

They were walking toward the fairy mound.

As a child, Ailene had longed to catch a glimpse of the Aos Sí. Yet now she had, panic fluttered up under her ribcage. Fear prickled across her skin. She was in grave danger here.

Ailene swallowed hard, cringing against Eòrna.
Thank the Gods, I never lit a fire.

She was also grateful that her pony had lowered himself onto the ground next to her. Ailene's pulse started to race. It was too late to run, too late to try and hide deeper in the hazel thicket.

She had nothing to do but pray that none of the Fair Folk looked her way.

The line of Fair Folk neared, and one by one, they disappeared into the mound. A doorway opened, and they stepped through it, until only one figure remained.

It was a woman with long golden hair that flowed down her back till it nearly reached the back of her knees. She wore a shimmering white gown.

Turning from the mound, the woman glided toward the thicket of trees.

Ailene's already pounding heart lurched. *Gods, no. She's seen me.*

The woman's face was beautiful, an ethereal loveliness with not the slightest imperfection upon it. Ailene wilted at the sight of such beauty, for she knew that the Fair Folk could be cruel. Ruith had told her many tales about how they meddled in the affairs of mortals, how they ruined lives merely for pleasure.

Next to her, the pony let out a weary sigh. He had not noticed the fairy's approach, and nor did he care.

When the woman was only a few yards away, she stopped. Despite her fair complexion, she had eyes as dark as a moonless night, deep and ageless. And when those black eyes fixed upon Ailene, she felt her body go cold.

"Bandruí." A cool, soft voice greeted her. The fairy's mouth did not move, yet Ailene heard her all the same. "We were hoping that one day our paths would cross."

Ailene did not answer. Fear had frozen her in place.

"You are welcome here." The voice continued. It had a gentle, beguiling note. "Come now, and join us."

Ailene swallowed. She wanted to reply, to send the woman on her way, yet her lips would not move, and her tongue felt leaden in her mouth.

The woman's beautiful lips curved, although those eyes remained fathomless, ancient. "We can take you away from all of this. We can end your struggle," she continued. The voice echoed in Ailene's head now, drowning out all other thoughts. "You are alone in this world, bandruí. But with us you will be where you belong."

The words were cruel and yet oddly beguiling. Dully, Ailene realized that the fairy woman had just cast an enchantment over her. And even as she fought it, Ailene was tempted.

Life had been a struggle of late for her—how had this fairy woman known that?

Muin.

Ailene jerked, as if someone had just slapped her across the face, and the enchantment lifted. She was out here in this desolate valley because of him. And if she did not catch up with Muin, did not warn him, he would die, as would many others.

To accept this woman's offer would mean death to all of them, including Ailene.

Life suddenly seemed incredibly precious. Ailene's heart beat fast, slamming against her ribs like a Bealtunn drum. It was a reminder of her mortality, of how fragile the line between life and death really was. She would not let this woman's sweet words draw her in.

"No." Ailene's voice came out in a croak. "I will remain here."

The fairy woman's head tilted. "You refuse our offer?"

Ailene straightened up, her hand gently moving in front of her in a warding gesture that Ruith had taught her. She wished that she carried salt with her, for these magical creatures would not dare to cross a line of salt.

The Fair Folk woman's black eyes narrowed. "Such an offer will never come your way again, bandruí." The voice turned ugly then, lowering to a hiss. "Next time our paths cross, there will be no choice. We will take you with us, whether you wish it or not."

And with that, the woman turned and glided away.

It was almost completely dark now, yet the woman glowed as if bathed in moonlight. She drifted toward the fairy mound, where an opening yawned before her, and then disappeared into the gloaming.

Ailene blinked, and the doorway into the mound had disappeared.

Long moments passed before Ailene released a long, shaky breath. The fairy's warning still rang in her ears, and despite the evening's chill, sweat bathed her skin under her layers of clothing.

That had been close—too close.

The Reaper had been breathing down her neck. With a jolt, Ailene realized that only the fact that she was a bandruí had saved her. Ruith had said that the Aos Sí were wary of seers.

The woman's message had been clear. The Fair Folk would not bother Ailene again tonight at least. However, the displeasure in the fairy's voice was a warning. It was best to move on from this place.

Heaving herself up off the ground, Ailene winced as her leg muscles protested. "Come on, lad." She gave Eòrna's reins a gentle tug, noting that her hands were shaking. Her heart still raced in the aftermath of her encounter. Suddenly, the rain, wind, and darkness did not bother her. "I think we'll find another spot to rest tonight."

Chapter Nineteen

Secrecy

EXHAUSTION WAS SETTLING upon Ailene in a heavy, smothering shroud, when she caught up with the army at last.

She had been traveling for over two days, taking only brief rests along the way. What little food she had brought had been consumed by the second morning of travel. Her belly was hollow and aching now, and she felt light headed.

However, she pressed on, her thoughts constantly returning to Muin. Worry tied her belly in knots.

Likewise, her pony was tiring. Eòrna carried his head low, his feathered feet thudding listlessly on the damp earth. She hated pushing him so hard, but she knew that her time was running out. The army of the united tribes would be about to begin their siege. She had to reach them before they did.

She had followed the army's trail with ease. The wet weather had left clear signs of their passing. The army had cut east before following the coastline of The Winged Isle farther east and then down, into the heart of occupied territory. On the way, they gave Kyleakin, and any other villages, a wide berth.

The Serpent would have taken over all the settlements in this area. It was best to keep a distance from all of them.

As such, the army had moved inland, to a wide valley that was covered in hawthorn and alders on its eastern edge, and boulders to the west.

She knew that she was traveling faster than the host she tracked, for a large group of ponies and warriors could not journey as swiftly as one pony, yet dread clawed its way up her throat with every furlong.

What if I'm too late?

When she crested a tall hill and spied smoke rising into the late afternoon sky, Ailene nearly wept with relief. The rain had ceased for the time being, speeding up her journey, although a chill wind still gusted in from the north-east.

Breathing hard, she brought Eòrna to a halt at the top of the hill and surveyed the wide valley below.

"Well done, lad." She leaned forward and stroked her pony's sweaty neck. "You have the heart of a giant."

In response, the gelding gave a soft whicker.

"Come on ... let's get you a nosebag of oats and a rub-down." Ailene urged the pony on. She guided Eòrna down the slope, between two large rocks, and met her first sentry shortly after.

"Who goes there?" A big man with wild dark hair, clad head-to-foot in leather, stepped out, blocking her path with a spear.

Ailene pulled up her pony, her gaze settling upon the man's face. Despite that she had walked amongst the warriors of the united tribes, blessing them before they departed Balintur, she did not recognize this man. From the suspicious expression the warrior wore, he did not know her either.

Drawing herself up, she fixed him with an imperious look she had often seen Ruith use in the past. "I'm Ailene ... The Eagle bandruí," she greeted him. "I have come with tidings for Varar and Galan. Please take me to them."

All conversation ceased when Ailene walked into the tent.

Halting in the doorway, she drew in a deep, steadying breath, her gaze sweeping over the interior.

She spotted Muin immediately. Her gaze was drawn to him against her will. All the other occupants of the tent faded into the background except for the tall warrior with long dark hair spilling over his broad shoulders.

Ailene would have smiled at him, if his expression had not been thunderous.

His storm-grey eyes were narrowed as he stared at her, his brawny arms folded across his muscular chest.

Muin, like the other warriors, would be wondering what she was doing here.

"Ailene," Galan's gruff voice intruded, drawing her gaze to where the Eagle chieftain stood near a glowing brazier in the center of the tent. Shock rippled over his face at the sight of her. Varar and Fina stood next to him, their expressions bemused. "Did you follow us?"

Ailene nodded.

"Alone?"

"Aye ... it was urgent so I couldn't wait." Ailene heard the tremor in her voice as her fear and exhaustion finally caught up with her. She could not give into it yet though.

"What is it?" Fina took a step toward her, alarm flaring in her eyes. "Have the bones told you something?"

Ailene shook her head. The telling bones sat in a pouch on her belt. She had not cast them since leaving Balintur. "I had a dream, a foretelling, of the siege of An Teanga." The words rushed out of Ailene. She fixed her attention on Varar then, who was watching her closely, a deep groove between his dark eyebrows. "How do you plan to take back the fort?"

"By water," he replied, his tone cautious. "Why?"

"How exactly?"

Varar's frown deepened. He glanced across at Galan, catching the Eagle chieftain's eye. Galan's lips compressed, before he gave a curt nod.

"We plan to swim in," The Boar chieftain replied after a pause. "After dark tomorrow evening. It'll be a new moon so no one will see us. We'll take the broch first."

Ailene swallowed, her pulse suddenly thundering in her ears. Stepping forward, she met Varar's gaze. "I've seen it," she said, her voice falling heavily in the now silent tent. "I watched you all swim up to the base of the broch on a moonless night and climb onto shore, knives in hand. But what you don't realize is that The Serpent has the broch well-defended. Their sentries guard the tower, but keep out of sight, hiding in the shadows lest an attack come from the water."

A shocked hush fell in the tent.

The two chieftains looked as if Ailene had just physically struck them across the face, whereas Calum of The Wolf and Moira of The Stag both gaped at her. Fina's face paled, while Muin's expression grew darker still.

Eventually, Fina broke the heavy silence. "How do you know all this?"

Ailene turned to her. "I told you ... I had a vision. The whole attack was as real to me as you are all now. I saw our warriors fight and fall." Her attention shifted to Galan and Varar once more. "If you try to take the broch from the water, the siege will fail."

※

"Muin, wait. I need to speak to you!"

Ailene ran after Muin as he strode away from the meeting tent. She could tell from the stiff set of his shoulders and the length of his stride that he was upset—yet she could not let him be.

Upon hearing his name called, Muin's step faltered. He then turned to Ailene, his face a stony mask.

Bracing herself, Ailene hurried up to him.

"What is it?" he greeted her, his tone clipped.

"I need to speak to you ... privately."

Muin's features shuttered. "There isn't anywhere private here," he replied, gesturing to the sea of hide tents surrounding him.

"Follow me then." Ailene gestured to the hillside behind them, where boulders rose into the early dusk. A thin mist had crept in, curling like crone's hair through the rocks. "We'll talk over there."

When Muin did not move, she stepped closer still to him. She longed to throw her arms around him and bury her face in his chest, yet she prevented herself. "Please ... this is important."

A shadow moved in his grey eyes, and a nerve flickered in his jaw, but after a long moment, Muin nodded.

Wordlessly, he followed her through the closely packed tents to the edge of the encampment. Her pulse pounding in her ears, Ailene led the way up the slope, passing the sentries halfway up. "You shouldn't go far," one of them warned. "Night is almost upon us."

"She won't," Muin replied gruffly. "I'm with her."

Ailene continued up the slope, leading Muin into a cluster of tall boulders that loomed overhead like tors. The wind shrieked across the hills this evening, yet the surrounding boulders offered some protection from it there.

"Why all the secrecy?" Muin asked when Ailene finally stopped and turned to him. He had that aloof mask in place, the one he had worn on the morning the army had departed from Balintur; it was an expression designed to keep her away from him.

Yet Ailene would not be silenced.

"I didn't want anyone to overhear us," she replied, holding his gaze; it was important that Muin believed her next words. "When I told the chieftains of my dream, there was an important part I left out ... a part that concerns you."

Muin's brow furrowed, and he took a slow step toward her. "Go on."

"I saw you climb out of the water and fight your way up to the base of the broch," she continued. "You fought savagely, but it was not enough. The Cruthini outnumbered you. I saw you go down ... an axe clove the back of your neck." Ailene broke off then. "The dream changed then into one I have had before ... one where I stand before your cairn, while your mother sings a lament for your death."

Muin's breathing had slowed, his brows knitting together. "You've had this dream before?"

Ailene nodded, her belly twisting in guilt. "While you were away on that scouting trip. I was terrified you would not return, and when you did, I thought it had been nothing more than a nightmare. However, when the vision returned it was even more vivid than the first time. And during that dream I saw how you fell."

Silence stretched between them for a few moments, before Muin eventually spoke. "You could have told me that in front of the others."

Ailene swallowed, nervousness rising within her. "I thought you'd prefer to be told alone. I know how reserved you are."

Tell him, a voice urged her. *Say the real reason you rode through storms to reach him.* However, her tongue suddenly felt as if it had fused to the roof of her mouth.

Muin cleared his throat. "Thank you for telling me this ... hopefully now that the others know, they will change their plans, and my death will not come to pass." His face had softened slightly, although his voice was flat.

Ailene's chest constricted, and she took a tentative step toward him. "Muin." Her voice caught as she said his name. "There's another reason why I wanted to speak to you alone. Will you listen to it?"

Chapter Twenty
I Can't Breathe Without You

MUIN INCLINED HIS head, his storm-grey gaze fixing upon her in a way that made Ailene's pulse race. "Aye," he replied softly. "What is it?"

Ailene drew in a shaky breath. Her body reacted so differently to Muin these days; it took some getting used to. She remembered all the times when they were children, and in their early teens, when they had swum naked together. Then she had been completely unselfconscious around him, as she had been that fateful evening that he had revealed his true feelings for her.

But now she was acutely aware of his presence, his masculinity.

Anxiety churned under her ribcage. Gods, how this scared her. She would rather face the Fair Folk again than this man.

"When I woke up from that ... that dream," she began stumbling over the words, "I was terrified." She paused there and wrapped her arms around her torso, hugging it tightly as she forced herself on. "All I could think about was that I ... I couldn't bear to lose you."

Muin went still. A beat of silence passed, before he spoke. "What are you saying, Ally?"

The use of his pet name for her made Ailene's breathing quicken. The timbre of his voice, low and husky, sent shivers of pleasure across her skin. How had she never noticed how sensual his voice was? This man's presence was so powerful, gentle yet strong, that it felt as if all the air had been sucked out of the narrow space between the boulders.

"I've been lying to myself." The words rushed out of her now. She had to say them, before her courage failed her completely. "I don't want to go through life without you. I don't want any other man. I can't breathe without you."

Surprise rippled across Muin's features. A moment later he moved toward her, stalking her.

Ailene stood firm, although her knees started to tremble. She was still terrified, yet she would not run from him. Not this time.

Muin reached her, and he raised a hand, gently cupping her cheek. "Do you mean that?"

Ailene swallowed. "Aye," she whispered.

He leaned in and kissed her then. Unlike the one he had given her two days earlier, which had swept upon her like an unexpected storm, this kiss was soft, tentative. He was testing her, making sure she meant her words.

The softness of his lips as they brushed hers, the rasp of his stubbled jaw as it brushed against her cheek, made Ailene's breathing catch.

How had she never noticed how good he smelled? Leather, fresh sweat, and virile male. Heat pooled through her lower belly, and with a sigh Ailene leaned into him, brushing her lips across his, mirroring his action.

Muin groaned low in his throat. His arms went around her, and he pulled Ailene against him, his mouth claiming hers hungrily now.

Ailene melted against him.

She would not hide from this, would not stop herself from living to the full.

Muin was life. The leashed power of his big body against hers, the hunger of his kiss, awakened a dormant sensation within Ailene.

Desire slammed into her, turning the cradle of her lower belly molten. Reaching up, she entwined her arms around Muin's neck, her lips parting as his tongue danced with hers.

"Gods," he groaned in her ear when they came up for air. "You taste incredible."

Ailene let out a soft laugh, which turned into a gasp as his tongue explored the shell of her ear before his lips trailed down the column of her throat. His touch left a line of fire in its wake. Reaching out, Ailene tangled her fingers in his hair. It was fine and soft, sliding through her fingers. She wanted that hair to trail over her naked body, over her swollen nipples.

She was keenly aware of her breasts then, pressed up against the hard wall of his chest. They felt constrained under layers of wool and leather; they ached for his touch.

As if sensing her growing frustration, Muin's hands slid down the curve of her back till they cupped her buttocks. Then he lifted her against him and carried her over to a boulder, pushing her back against it.

And there he kissed her again.

He kissed her until she gasped for breath, until her lips stung, until the tender skin of her chin burned from the rasp of his stubble. Ailene did not care, did not want him ever to stop. Her tongue tangled with his as she strained toward him. Their bodies entwined, and Ailene could feel the hard column of his arousal pressing against her belly.

A memory returned to her, of that night in her hut after the council, when Muin had stood up to leave. The erection that had strained against his tight breeches had been impressive. It had been an effort not to stare at it. At unguarded moments ever since, she had dwelled on his reaction to her and had even caught herself looking at his groin once or twice.

Heat had flowed through her when she had, swiftly followed by embarrassment. This was Muin, her best friend. She had not wanted to see him that way.

But there was no embarrassment now. Ailene ground her hips against his, her hands exploring the muscular breadth of his shoulders, before they slid down to his chest.

His heart hammered under her palm.

Eventually, Muin pulled back, breathing hard. Ailene's gaze went to his mouth; his lips were swollen too from their wild kisses. His eyes were hooded and had darkened to a dark iron-grey. His high cheek bones were flushed.

Ailene ran her hands down the wall of his chest and over the muscled ridges of his belly. However, when she reached the ties to his plaid breeches, he caught her by the wrists.

"I'm going to make love to you," he growled out the words. "But not out here ... I want to take you naked ... and I want to take my time."

The promise made Ailene's breathing hitch. Hunger pulsed through her with each beat of her heart, and her core ached.

Muin stepped back from her, his lips curving in a slow smile that caused excitement to rear up within Ailene. He then caught her hand, his fingers entwining through hers.

"Follow me," he murmured.

Ailene stood in the tent, smoothing her palms against her thin linen tunic.

Muin had left her in here, with a wash bowl and drying cloths, before disappearing. Alone, Ailene had suddenly gotten nervous. All of this was happening so fast. One moment she had been baring her soul to Muin, the next she was in his arms.

She was not used to acting so brazenly.

The tent was bigger than most—Muin's rank as a chieftain's son afforded him better lodgings than others, who crawled into cramped tents at the end of a day's march.

This tent's roof was high enough for a tall man to stand upright. Deerskin covered the ground, and a pile of furs lay to the back. A brazier sat in the heart of the tent, a lump of peat glowing there. The air was warm and scented with the pungent aroma of peat-smoke, despite the slit in the roof to let the smoke out.

Trembling with anticipation, Ailene had yanked off her boots, stepped out of her skirt, and stripped off her woolen tunic. After that, she undid her vest so that she was clad only in a thin sleeveless tunic that reached mid-thigh.

Muin had left her a bowl of steaming water, and a cake of lye scented with rosemary, to wash with. Relief had filtered over her at the sight of it; after two days of hard travel, she longed to wash the grime off her skin.

Ailene washed quickly, the feel of the warm water against her already sensitive skin heightening her arousal. The tender flesh between her thighs throbbed now, and when she washed herself there, she let out a soft whimper of need.

She hoped Muin would return soon.

He took his time.

Ailene was standing next to the brazier, resisting the urge to pace the tent, when a tall figure ducked inside.

Muin let the flap fall closed behind him and moved toward her, stopping when they were a few feet apart. His gaze raked down her body, taking in her unbound hair and the gauzy material of her tunic that Ailene knew was virtually transparent.

His lips parted slightly, his gaze darkening.

Never taking his eyes off her, Muin heeled off his boots and started to unlace his vest.

Ailene swallowed, a blend of excitement and nerves fluttering in the cradle of her hips. "This is a nice tent," she said, before inwardly cursing herself for saying something so inane. Nervousness had made her babble. "You don't have to share it?"

Muin favored her with a lopsided smile. "Aye ... but I've told Aaron he can sleep elsewhere tonight."

Chapter Twenty-one

Take Your Pleasure

MUIN SHUCKED OFF his vest and started unlacing his breeches.

Ailene's heart began to pound as she watched him. Muin undressing was the most erotic thing she had ever seen. The soft light of the brazier played across the strong lines of his body. The mark of the Eagle on his chest rippled as he moved.

Then Muin let his breeches fall and stepped out of them—and Ailene momentarily stopped breathing.

He was magnificent.

His shaft, strong and sculpted, strained up against his ridged belly. And as Ailene stared at it, Muin wrapped his hand around his thick girth and gave his rod a long, sensual stroke.

Ailene's knees nearly buckled under her.

Gods, how she wanted him. She ached to fall to her knees before him and take that rod in her hands, to draw it deep into her mouth till he groaned.

The thought shocked her.

She was not a maid, yet she felt as inexperienced as one right now. Her union with Fingal had been brief and rough. She remembered his shaft as a swollen, pulsing thing that had hurt her.

She had not yearned to touch it, not like she did now with Muin.

A low groan escaped Ailene, frustration and desire overwhelming her.

Muin was suddenly on her. One moment he had been standing a few feet away, lazily stroking himself as he watched her, the next Ailene was in his arms, and his mouth and hands were everywhere.

Ailene inhaled the scent of him. His warm skin was damp and smelled faintly of lye and rosemary. He too had bathed.

Grasping the hem of Ailene's tunic, he hauled it up, over her head, his mouth fastening greedily upon her breasts when she raised her arms high.

Ailene gasped, leaning into him. She closed her eyes as he suckled her, pleasure darting straight down from her swollen nipple to her core. Throwing her head back, she groaned his name.

Muin shifted toward the furs then, drawing her with him. He seated himself upon them. Ailene knelt astride him as he continued to feast upon her breasts. And as he did so, his strong hands explored her body, stroking down her ribs, to the soft curve of her belly, the dip of her waist, and the swell of her buttocks.

His fingers brushed the nest of dark curls between her thighs, and Ailene let out a soft whimper. She ached for him to touch her there. Even so, it was a shock when he slid a long, thick finger inside her. She was tight, and the sensation made her gasp. Then, as his thumb stroked her, she whimpered once more.

"I love the noises you make when I touch you, mo chridhe." Muin's voice was low and husky.

My heart.

Ailene let out a long, shuddering sigh. She could barely think, let alone form coherent sentences, not when his finger now slowly slid in and out of her. She trembled against him, and then moments later she bucked against his hand, a cry escaping her. "Muin!"

She reached down, her fingers wrapping around his shaft. It was hot and hard, the skin unbelievably smooth. She stroked his length, mirroring his earlier gesture.

It was Muin's turn to groan then, his head falling back, his eyelids fluttering as she pleasured him.

And then Ailene could not take it anymore. She had to have him inside her, or she felt as if her chest would explode from want.

She lowered herself to him, positioning his shaft at her entrance. The sensation of him sliding inside her was almost too much. He was big, and this position meant that she took him deep. Yet Ailene did not falter; she sank down upon him, impaling herself to the root.

Her breathing was coming in short pants when their gazes met and held.

She felt full, stretched to the limit, a deep pulsing ache of pleasure flowering inside her.

Muin leaned back on his hands, his gaze never leaving hers. "Ride me, Ailene," he growled. "Take your pleasure."

Heat flooded across Ailene's chest at these words. She had never realized Muin had this side to him. She felt completely safe with him, and yet at the same time the predatory gleam in his eye gave their coupling a thrill of danger.

Obeying him, Ailene rotated her hips, groaning as pleasure throbbed through her loins. Biting her lower lip, she began to ride him, rocking back and forward. She slid up and down his thick, slick rod.

Cries filled the tent, and Ailene was vaguely aware they were hers. The sensation of him filling her, stroking her deep inside, took her to the brink. She shuddered against him, gasping.

A heartbeat later Muin reared up, his arms fastening around her. He flipped Ailene onto her back, lifted her legs over his shoulders, and drove into her. His face was savage, his eyes black with lust.

The sight of him losing control shattered the last of Ailene's restraint. She arched up toward him, writhing as he thrust into her. Her cries grew wilder, louder. The whole camp would be able to hear them now, yet Ailene did not care.

The only thing that mattered was the pair of them.

Muin took her to the edge, and then together they toppled over it, both crying each other's name as they came.

"Gods, I can't move."

Ailene huffed a laugh against Muin's chest. "What? Have I injured you?"

"Only temporarily ... I hope."

Ailene smiled, her fingers tracing designs across the sculpted lines of Muin's chest. He was beautifully built, stronger and broader than many other men. Up close, she noted how intricate his eagle tattoo was. She remembered when he'd had it done. Talor had teased him for days about the fact that Muin had not had the mark of The Eagle inked upon his arm like most folk.

The young warrior, just out of boyhood, had wanted something different.

Muin had always been his own man.

Ailene's fingers slid down his right arm then, to the leather bracelet studded with tiny turquoise stones around his wrist. "You still wear this?"

"Aye," Muin replied softly. "I've never taken it off."

Ailene's smile widened. She had spent days finding all the stones for the bracelet and weaving them securely into the leather. It warmed her heart that he was so attached to it.

"We're meeting again tomorrow morning," Muin said after a long pause. "Varar and my father will change their plans."

Relief suffused Ailene at these words; she had known that Varar and Galan would not be able to ignore her warning, but it was reassuring to hear Muin confirm her hopes.

"Will you tell them about what I saw ... in your future?" Ailene asked.

She felt Muin's big body tense against hers. "Is there any point? If we change our attack, then doesn't the future change too?"

"Aye," Ailene admitted cautiously. She propped herself up on Muin's chest then, meeting his gaze. "But maybe you shouldn't fight tomorrow."

Muin's mouth lifted at the corners. "That's like suggesting I stop breathing, Ally. Of course I will fight."

Ailene swallowed. "But what if I'm wrong? What if even changing the attack won't save you?"

He caught her hand and raised it to his lips, kissing her palm. "Then, it's my time to go."

Ailene's pulse quickened. "How can you be so fatalistic? Don't you want to live?"

His eyes shadowed, and his grip tightened upon her hand. "Of course I do." He reached up with his free hand, tracing her cheek with his fingertips. "But you know as well as I that the will of the Gods can't be escaped. The Reaper comes for us when *he* decides. When my time in this world is at an end, I will have little say in the matter."

His voice faded away then, and the pair of them watched each other for a long moment. Muin's mouth quirked. "Don't look so worried, love," he murmured. "I'll not be reckless tomorrow; I'll not throw my life away." He traced her full lower lip with the pad of his thumb. "Not when I have so much to live for."

Hearing his reassurance, the panic that had tightened into a fist around Ailene's heart eased.

Holding her gaze, Muin's mouth curved into a smile.

Ailene gave him an arch look. "What are you looking so pleased about, Muin mac Galan?"

"I can feel my strength returning," he replied, a wicked gleam lighting in his eyes. In one swift movement, he rolled over so that Ailene was pinned under him. "And that means we're done resting."

Chapter Twenty-two
Let Them Come to Us

GALAN MAC MUIN frowned down at the map Varar had drawn in the dirt. "Taking the broch from the water was our best idea," he admitted. "Getting in any other way will be much harder."

A few feet away, Varar glanced up from where he had hunkered down to scratch out the outline of his fort. The group had gathered in a clearing in front of the meeting tent. A pale sunrise greeted them, mist wreathing the surrounding hills. "I agree," he murmured, "but with your seer's foretelling, I will not risk an attack from the water."

"I wasn't suggesting that," Galan replied, his brows knitting together.

Watching the two chieftain's interact, Muin tensed. His father and Varar were allies these days, although there was still a lingering tension between them. Varar was much younger than Galan, and there were times when Muin realized that his father chafed at having to share leadership of this army with him. Even if it was Varar's stronghold they were about to take back.

Muin's lips thinned. It was no surprise then that his father stone-walled his own son every time he came up with a suggestion. Galan liked being the one to lead.

Heaving a deep breath, Muin stepped forward. "I have an idea."

Both chieftains glanced toward Muin, as did Calum and Moira, who stood opposite him. Fina flanked her husband, her grey eyes narrowing as she met Muin's eye. Muin suppressed the urge to smile; she was likely remembering what had happened last time he had spoken up during a council.

Muin cast a look over his shoulder then, at where Ailene stood a few feet behind him, silently watching the discussion.

She wore her formal 'bandruí' countenance this morning; a different woman from the lusty lover who had ridden him, her cries spilling out into the night. Lying with Ailene had been better than his wildest imaginings.

Of course, he had spent many nights over the past few years pleasuring himself as he imagined what it would be like to lie with Ailene. But he had never expected her to be so wild, or for his own response to be so unfettered. She completely shattered his self-control. He felt like a different man this morning; even the grey dawn had a rosy glow in the aftermath of the night he had spent with her.

Their gazes fused for an instant, and then Muin turned back to where his father and Varar were watching him intently.

Muin moved forward and hunkered down next to Varar. "Our numbers more or less equal theirs," he began. "The attack from the water was only going to work if the warriors inside the fort were evenly distributed ... but we now know that they aren't. Most of them are guarding the broch itself."

He then took the stick The Boar chieftain passed him and drew an arrow outside the north-eastern perimeter. "I suggest we attack the village first from this direction. We won't be hemmed in there ... and it will draw the warriors out of the broch." Muin glanced up, his gaze fusing with his father's. "Let them come to us."

Silence fell over the clearing. Muin watched Calum and Moira exchange glances, before a smile stretched Varar's face. The Boar chieftain glanced over at Galan. "I like this plan."

"So do I," Fina spoke up. "I think it might work."

Muin continued to hold his father's gaze. Galan's expression was stern, his face hawkish. For a moment Muin feared that The Eagle chieftain would disagree with him, and then Galan smiled.

It transformed his father's face—and Muin realized how rarely he saw his father smile these days. Life for The Eagle had been hard of late, and Muin knew how much the duty weighed upon his father's shoulders. Galan had always taken responsibility for things that were out of his control. It had wounded him to take his people from Dun Ringill. He would not be himself again until they returned to their home.

"It is a wise plan," he said finally. "Well done, son."

The murmur of voices, punctuated by the rasp and clang of iron, shattered the morning's stillness. Ailene walked through the camp, weaving her way through tightly-packed clusters of hide tents. She passed a group of warriors who were painting each other's faces and limbs with woad.

The siege of An Teanga approached.

Ailene waved to one or two warriors, but left them to their preparations. She had some time alone, for Muin was taken up finalizing the details of the siege with Varar and Galan.

Up ahead she spotted Tea seated upon a rock in front of the tent she and Galan shared. She was sharpening her sword. Tea had come on the campaign, not to fight in the coming siege, but to oversee the camp once the other warriors left. Should the battle go ill, it would be up to Tea to get the few warriors who had remained behind in the rear-guard to safety.

Spying Ailene, Tea stopped sharpening her blade and raised a hand, waving Ailene over.

Heat rose in Ailene's cheeks as she approached. She had not cared if the whole camp heard her and Muin's lovemaking the night before. But suddenly, in the cold light of day, she felt embarrassed. She had made a lot of noise.

Her face burned when she saw Tea was smiling, a knowing glint in her midnight-blue eyes.

"Don't look so worried," Tea greeted Ailene with a soft laugh. "I'm happy for you both."

Ailene let out a slow exhale, relief filtering through her.

Tea's expression grew soft then. "Muin's only ever loved you, Ailene. There's never been anyone else for him."

Ailene went still. "You knew how he felt?"

Tea's mouth curved. "Of course ... a mother always knows."

Deep in thought, Ailene returned to Muin's tent.

Tea's words had left an impression upon her. It seemed that she was the only one who had been blind to Muin's feelings. She had not welcomed the vision of Muin's death, yet it had forced her to face how she really felt for him. Following Muin here was the best decision she had ever made.

The brazier had long gone out, and the sight of the pile of furs, where they had lain together, made Ailene's breathing quicken. She could not wait to couple with Muin again, to curl against him in the aftermath and hear the steady thud of his heart against her ear.

Digging into the pouch at her waist, Ailene withdrew her telling bones.

She had not cast them in days, not with everything that had happened. But it was time now. She needed to know what the coming days would bring—especially since the battle for An Teanga would begin after dark.

Ailene knelt on the deerskins and tested the weight of the bones in her hand. Then, inhaling deeply and whispering a plea to the Gods, she cast the bones. They tumbled across the deerskin, clinking and clattering together until they came to rest upon the red deer pelt.

Watching them, Ailene's breathing caught.

The mark of The Boar had rolled far from the other bones, making it impossible for her to gain any knowledge from its position. But it was not that which made foreboding tickle the back of Ailene's neck.

Not again.

The mark of the Eagle had fallen next to the sickle and The Hag. The bones refused to change their story. Dark times still lay ahead for her people. But even more worrying, there were two other bones that had rolled together.

The mark of the crow had fallen directly above a crescent moon.

Ailene sat back on her heels. "The Death Tide," she whispered.

She had never cast such a combination before, although Ruith had explained the meaning of these two marks to Ailene years earlier.

"The Reaper will sharpen his sickle and stride out into the world." Ailene's hoarse whisper filled the tent. "A red tide will rise, and when it recedes, it will leave death in its wake."

Ailene's throat constricted. She ran a hand over her face, the other hand splaying across her breast where her heart now pounded. This was the last thing she needed to see, not now, not right before her people went into battle.

Her belly contracted. "Calm down," she hissed to herself, scooping up the telling bones and depositing them back in their pouch. "Aye, death is coming ... but the bones do not tell me who will die. It may be that this sign is not for us at all, but for The Serpent."

Counselling herself aloud calmed her, kept the panic at bay. Ailene rose to her feet, sweat suddenly beading her skin.

What should I do?

Her first instinct was to go to Galan and Varar, to tell them of the 'Death Tide'. However, she checked herself. Was that wise? Would they even call off the attack based on such a warning, especially since the sign had not fallen near any of the markings of their tribes? The sign, although terrible, was not specific in its meaning.

No, I won't tell them ... not even Muin.

She did not want to risk panicking them, or worse still, lowering morale. Muin's plan was a sound one, and they needed to go into battle confident, not with the shadow of doom trailing over them.

Ailene dragged in a deep breath, her resolve hardening. She needed to trust her own instincts.

This time she would remain silent.

Chapter Twenty-three

Turning the Tide

Balintur
Territory of The Eagle

"ANY SIGN OF the enemy?"

Talor turned from his station upon the wall, to see his half-sister Bonnie approach. Small, with a pert, heart-shaped face and long braided hair, she wore little more than two bands of leather covering her breasts and loins, despite the icy wind that howled down the valley surrounding Balintur.

"None," he replied. "The Serpent won't be slithering in today ... with any luck, they're finding this isle too cold."

Bonnie snorted. "They looked hardy enough to me ... I've never seen such big warriors." She paused then, frowning. "Da told me that war drove them from the mainland."

"Aye," Talor grunted. "That Boar traitor who lives with them suggested they move here instead."

Bonnie's eyes gleamed. "A decision they're likely regretting."

"And if they aren't ... they soon will be," Talor replied, his gaze sweeping over the bleak hills that rolled south in the direction of Dun Ringill. The end of his watch was drawing to a close, and he was looking forward to retiring to his hut and downing some warmed mead. After a moment he glanced back at his sister. "What are you doing up here ... you're not on the watch today."

"Ma wants to know if you're joining us for supper this eve?"

"It depends," Talor replied with a grin. "What's she cooking?"

"Blood sausage and eggs."

Talor's mouth filled with saliva at this news. His step-mother, Eithni, knew he adored blood sausage. She would have sent Bonnie out to find him especially. Guilt arrowed through him then. Since coming to live at Balintur, he had been so taken up with preparations for war that he now spent little time with his kin.

The round-house that his father and Eithni shared with his two half-sisters, Eara and Bonnie, was cramped enough as it was without him taking up extra space. It had been a relief to move in with Muin. But Eithni had missed him—and this supper was her way of letting him know that a visit was long overdue.

"Alright then." Talor unslung the heavy fur cloak he wore around his shoulders and stepped close to his sister, casting it around her. "Here, lass. You'll freeze up here without this."

Bonnie snorted and tried to shrug the cloak off. "Nonsense. I don't feel the cold."

Talor kept his hands firmly pressed on the young woman's shoulders. At sixteen, Bonnie could outdo him when it came to pig-headedness. "The wind is cold enough to freeze a man's cods. You're wearing this."

Bonnie laughed. "Lucky for me, I'm not a man."

However, she did not try and remove the cloak again. Talor resumed his post upon the wall. A narrow walkway, only wide enough for one warrior at a time, ran around the edge of Balintur's high stone walls.

Without his fur mantle, the wind bit through his clothing and chilled his skin. The thought of joining his family for supper and warming his hands by the fire certainly appealed.

"Has Ailene returned yet?" he asked after a pause.

"I haven't seen her," Bonnie replied. "Isn't it a strange time of year to go foraging for herbs?"

Talor frowned. "Aye," he murmured. His cousin's mysterious trip north bothered him. Before he retired for the evening he would seek out Ailene. If she had not returned, he would send out a search party after her.

Glancing at Bonnie's profile, he found his sister looking south, her brow furrowed. He sensed then that her thoughts were not on Ailene, but on the fort that lay to the south—the home they had been forced to abandon. "I miss Dun Ringill," she murmured. She shifted her gaze to him then, her hazel eyes that were so much like her mother's shadowed. "Will we ever get it back?"

"Aye, lass," Talor replied without a moment's hesitation. "Come spring, we'll drive those bastards out and send them off this isle with their tails tucked between their legs. They'll wish they'd never crossed the water."

His sister's eyes lightened, and her mouth curved. "You're always so certain of things. How is that possible?"

Talor raised an eyebrow. He knew he had inherited his father's stubborn, forceful nature. He had no memory of his mother, Luana, for she had died shortly after giving birth to him. However, his father had told him that she was a sweet-natured woman who laughed often. Apart from her sea-blue eyes, which Talor had inherited from her, there did not appear to be much of his mother in him.

"There are some things I must be sure about," he replied after a pause, "and returning to Dun Ringill is one of them." He swung his attention south once more, to where tawny hills rose against the cloudy sky. "Those Serpent bastards took our home. I'm going to enjoy ripping it from them."

He glanced back to see his sister's expression was as fierce as his. Like Talor, Bonnie had inherited her father's warrior spirit. Only wee Eara took after her mother. Even though she was still young, the lass had already taken an interest in Eithni's healing herbs and potions.

"So will I," Bonnie replied.

---

*Occupied territory
North-east of An Teanga*

Ailene stretched up and kissed Muin. "Watch your back out there," she murmured against his lips.

Muin cupped Ailene's face with his hands, his mouth slanting across hers. When he pulled back, he was smiling. "I always do."

"Make a special effort to do so today," she replied, staring deep into his eyes. "I know you've changed your plans so my vision should no longer come to pass ... but even so, the Gods are fickle."

Muin's eyes were warm as he drew her against him. "I understand your worries ... and I will heed them."

Ailene was aware then that they were drawing a few glances and smiles from the surrounding warriors. Two men nearby were elbowing each other, grins plastered on their faces.

Muin ignored them, although Ailene could feel her cheeks warming under their scrutiny. It was hard to keep your affairs a secret in a community like theirs. Few events went unnoticed among her people.

Around them the light was starting to fade. It was late afternoon, and the wind had finally died—as it often did at the day's end. A helmet of grey hung over the land, and there was a watchful feel to the sky, almost as if the

Gods were indeed looking down, wondering what they would witness next.

The Death Tide ... maybe I should say something?

Ailene's spine prickled then as she wrestled with her conscience once more. She stepped back from Muin, her gaze sweeping about the amassed crowd. The warriors of the united tribes— Eagles, Wolves, Stags, and Boar— were about to depart. All were heavily armed, streaks of blue painting their faces and exposed limbs. They looked dangerous—they looked unbeatable.

Ailene swallowed, pushing down her desire to share her worries with Muin.

I hope they are.

They approached An Teanga on foot, leaving their ponies behind at the camp in the sheltered valley some furlongs distant.

Muin stalked through the gathering shadows, just a few feet behind Varar and Fina. Galan walked to Muin's left, with Aaron beside him. His younger brother glared at the settling dusk, his shoulders stiff with tension. The Battle of Bodach's Throat had been Aaron's first taste of battle. This was to be his second.

Their father had drawn his sword. His brow was furrowed, his face set in harsh, determined lines. Having fought alongside his father numerous times now, Muin knew that The Eagle chieftain was lethal in battle. A killing fury lay beneath his calm, controlled exterior; a fury that Muin also shared. He often forgot himself when the battle rage came.

Up ahead the squat outline of the broch rose against the darkening sky. Soon they would reach the high wooden palisade that ringed the village—and the first sentries.

Varar had sent a handful of his warriors ahead, to deal with those outlying guards.

A short while later they passed the fallen Serpent sentries: three men lay face-down in the dirt.

Approaching the fort from the north-east was the wisest choice. They had more cover here, for a patchwork of tilled fields stretched around most of the hillside beyond An Teanga, making it difficult to get close to the walls without being seen. On this hillside, bordered by a rocky shore, gorse and bramble grew in unruly bushes, obscuring them.

During their meeting earlier in the day, Varar had mentioned that this slope had always been An Teanga's weak spot. His father, Urcal, had kept the slope cleared, for he had known that it could conceal the approach of warriors from the north—but in the last year the scrub had grown back. And The Serpent warriors who now held the fort had not thought to clear it away.

Even so, Varar led the warriors cautiously forward. Four furlongs back from the village perimeter, he raised a hand, forcing all of them to stop and crouch low.

Muin knew why. It was not quite dark enough yet.

Fires had just been lit on the walls, and he spied the outlines of figures up there, watching over the land beyond.

They would not move again until night had completely fallen.

Muin shifted position as his thigh muscles started to cramp, and for the first time since leaving the encampment, he allowed his thoughts to shift from what lay ahead, to what he had left behind.

He still could not believe what had transpired between him and Ailene.

When she had led him up to the boulders to talk, he had felt sick with dread.

And then, in an instant, everything had changed.

Something had awakened in Ailene in the past few days, an awareness of him that had maybe been there for years but had lain dormant, hidden by a complex net of fears. Muin had been so sure she did not want him. She had not recoiled when he had kissed her back in Balintur, but she had not welcomed his touch either. He had thought his feelings were one-sided, and yet when he pulled her into his arms in the shelter of those boulders, Ailene had responded with a hunger that matched his own.

And then when they had come together in the privacy of his tent, every fantasy that Muin had ever had about Ailene had been realized.

Muin blinked, forcing thoughts of the comely seer from his mind.

There would be plenty of time for him to enjoy her fire again, for them to discover each other as lovers rather than friends. But now he had to focus on taking back An Teanga.

Before him, Varar slowly rose to his feet, a dark outline against the night that had settled around them.

Muin followed suit and, slowly, the warriors crept toward the north gate, weaving in between clumps of gorse and broom.

Varar slowed his breathing, the fingers of his right hand flexing around the hilt of his sword, while he adjusted his shield with his left.

Not long now.

The north gate hove into view, its wood and iron bulk illuminated by the glow of surrounding braziers. The gate was closed, and a line of bulky, leather-clad figures stood before it.

In the darkness, Muin allowed himself a cold smile.

In a few moments those Cruthini were about to taste iron. This was it, the moment the tide would start to turn against Cathal mac Calum and his horde. Once An Teanga fell, so would the rest of the occupied territory.

A heartbeat later Varar and Fina moved, streaking across the last stretch of ground to where the scrub ended and the gate rose.

Muin followed.

Chapter Twenty-four
A Formidable Foe

MUIN YANKED HIS sword out of the throat of the warrior he had just brought down and glanced up.

For the first time since the attack had begun, he'd had a moment to breathe, a moment to take in his surroundings properly.

Battle fury pulsed through him, although Muin could feel the shadow of exhaustion looming through it.

The Serpent were a formidable foe.

Cuts and grazes stung his arms and shoulders where the enemy blades had brushed him. The injuries were shallow, yet the men and women who had wielded those pikes, axes, and swords had been filled with the same killing rage as Muin.

His body ached, and his temples pounded. He had never fought so hard.

They had taken the village, and as hoped, the initial siege had drawn the bulk of The Serpent fighting force out of the broch. The fighting was now concentrated in the space between the armory and stable complex and the wide grassy area before the broch itself.

A huge man with braided chestnut hair ran at Muin, roaring like a stag in rutting season. He swung two axes, his face twisted into a savage mask.

Muin ducked out of his way before going in low and kicking the warrior's legs out from under him. It was a move that Talor had perfected over the years, and one that he had taught Muin.

It was the best way to bring down a dangerous opponent.

The warrior cursed as he fell, yet despite that he was big, he rolled easily and sprang to his feet.

Muin was ready for him. He attacked, getting in close so that the Cruthini could not raise his axes against him. Such weapons needed reach. In close quarters, both men drew their fighting knives.

Fire burned across Muin's left shoulder as his opponent's blade grazed him. The pain galvanized him, banished the battle fatigue that had started to press down upon Muin.

With a roar, he head-butted his opponent and slashed the man's wrist. The warrior grunted, blood pulsing from the wound as he grappled with Muin. It was a serious wound, for Muin had severed an artery, yet the warrior was strong enough to fight on for a while yet.

Muin twisted in his opponent's grip, as the man grappled for his face, attempting to gouge his eyes out. Muin drove his elbow up into the warrior's throat and crushed his wind-pipe. The man gasped, his gaze springing wide.

An instant later Muin had buried a knife in his opponent's throat.

Panting, Muin pushed himself up off the warrior, retrieved his weapons, and pushed on into the fray. The fighting had reached its peak now, and he saw that indeed, the battle had turned in his own people's favor.

Eventually, only a handful of Serpent warriors were left, and those who did not run screaming at their opponents, preferring to die than be taken captive, dropped their weapons and fell to their knees, arms raised.

Relief slammed into Muin as he bent over to regain his breath. They had hit the fort hard, giving the enemy no quarter. His plan of attack had worked.

Moving through the crowd, Muin checked to see who among his own were injured. Like Muin, Aaron was splattered with blood, his bare arms scored with cuts. Although his brother's face was ashen, he flashed Muin a victory grin.

"It's done," Aaron called out, his voice raspy with fatigue. "An Teanga is ours!"

Muin grinned back, before he shifted his attention to the warriors around them. Varar and Fina had also survived the battle. They were both blood-splattered but uninjured, although there were too many of the united tribes lying dead across the ground for Muin's liking.

Nausea closed Muin's throat as the rage of battle dimmed. He knew that they could not have taken back the fort without spilling some of their own people's blood. Even so, the sight sickened him.

A few yards away, he saw a big man finish off his Cruthini opponent. As Muin had predicted, Donnan mac Muir, Gavina's husband, had survived the battle.

Muin kept moving, his gaze sweeping the bodies scattered around him.

His heart leaped when he saw that one of his friends, Alban, was among the fallen. The warrior lay sprawled on his front. Hunkering down, Muin turned him over. Green eyes stared up sightlessly; his throat had been slit from ear to ear.

Grief constricted Muin's throat. Alban was just two winters his elder. They had grown up in Dun Ringill together, had trained together, run patrols together. Alban had left a wife and two daughters back in Balintur.

Reaching out, Muin gently shut his friend's eyes. "Go to your long sleep, brother," he whispered.

"Da!" Muin's chin jerked up to see Aaron elbow his way through the crowd to where Galan had sunk to his knees. He had been fighting near the steps to the broch, the bodies of his opponents littered around him.

Leaving Alban, Muin followed his brother to their father's side.

"I'm fine," Galan grunted, attempting to push Aaron away as he tried to help him to his feet.

"No, you're not," Muin countered, taking hold of his father's opposite arm. An axe blade had caught him on his left flank, just below the ribs. Blood ran down his leather breeches.

Galan muttered a curse under his breath, yet his face had gone the color of milk, and he was sweating. Muin knew he was in agony. Together, the two brothers helped him to the steps, where they lowered him onto the stone. The light of the nearby brazier played across the strained lines of The Eagle chieftain's face.

Varar and Fina moved past, climbing the steps into the broch, bringing a company of fighters with them.

There would likely still be some Serpent warriors inside, but the battle was won now. The rest of the fort had fallen. The rest of the warriors of the united tribes were combing the village, taking captives and checking on their own injured.

Shouting echoed out of the entrance to the broch, shattering the night once more.

Muin glanced up, frowning. "I'm going in there to help," he said to his brother. "Stay with Da."

"I don't need to be watched over," Galan growled. He went to rise, as if he too planned to join the final battle for An Teanga. But his eyelids fluttered, and he sagged. He would have toppled sideways if Aaron had not caught him.

"Stay with him," Muin repeated, meeting Aaron's eye.

His brother nodded.

Without another word, Muin sheathed his sword, drew his still bloodied knife, and rushed up the steps into the broch.

Ailene pushed the thin strand of thread made from stretched and dried sheep's intestines through the wound in Galan's side, before knotting it. Then, drawing back slightly, she surveyed her work.

The wound was long and deep, yet she had cleaned it first with strong wine before doing sutures as Eithni had taught her. It was not as neat a job as the healer would have done, but Ailene was glad that she'd assisted Eithni so often over the years. Galan could not wait till they reached Balintur for assistance.

In Eithni's absence her skills would have to do.

"What do you think?"

Ailene glanced right to see Muin watching her, his grey eyes shadowed.

Galan lay upon a pile of furs, in what had once been Varar's alcove. Unlike Dun Ringill, An Teanga was built on two levels. The top floor was for the chieftain and his kin.

"I think I've done all I can for now," she replied with a tired smile. "The wound is clean ... once we get back to Balintur, Eithni will be able to take care of him properly.'

"She would be pleased with your skills, I think," Tea spoke up. She sat at her husband's side, still grasping his hand.

When Ailene had washed the wound with wine, Galan had let out a strangled cry and fainted. He still lay unconscious now. It had been for the best anyway, for it had made sewing the sutures much easier.

The soft light of the cressets burning on the stone wall next to the furs illuminated the worry on Tea's face. Behind her, Aaron looked on, his expression sickly. He had looked ready to faint when they had removed his father's leather vest to reveal the full extent of his wound.

"From what I can see, the blade didn't pierce his gut," Ailene continued. The three of them looked so worried that she wanted to ease their concerns. "Galan was very lucky."

Tea nodded, her midnight blue eyes gleaming. "Thank you, lass," she whispered.

Descending the stone steps, Ailene took in the crowd of men and women that sat at the long tables below. Their voices, jubilant in the aftermath of victory, shook the rafters.

Another smile curved Ailene's mouth.

Relief suffused her, the sensation so strong she almost felt light-headed from it. After the army had departed from camp, she had been unable to settle. She could not stay by the fire pit and keep Tea company, nor could she return to the tent where she and Muin had spent the night before. Instead, she had circled the camp, a fur mantle wrapped around her shoulders, her thoughts churning.

When the riders had reached them just before dawn, bringing news of a successful attack, her legs had nearly given out under her.

There had been many injured warriors to tend to—Galan among them—but now that the noon meal was upon them, she desperately needed to sit for a while, and eat and drink. She would not be much assistance to those she was tending if she collapsed.

Taking a seat at one of the long tables, Ailene shared a smile with the woman next to her before reaching for a piece of bread. She then cut off a wedge of aged sheep's cheese, sliced up a small sweet onion to go with it, and fell upon her simple meal.

She was just washing it down with a gulp of ale, when Muin took a seat opposite.

Their gazes met and fused for a long moment. Ailene drank him in, grateful to see that apart from the odd graze and shallow cuts that she had dressed, he was unhurt. His face, however, bore lines of exhaustion and strain. He had not slept for two days, and it was starting to show.

"You need to rest," she said, pouring him a cup of ale. "You look ready to drop."

Muin winced. "Aye ... and I feel it too." He glanced up at the raised platform at the far end of the hall, where Varar and Fina sat side by side at a long table. "But it's good to see The Boar chieftain and his wife taking their rightful seats."

Ailene nodded as she too took in the happy couple as they spoke together, heads bent close. Varar's carven chair was magnificent. Made of polished oak and high-backed, it had two carved boar heads for armrests.

Once again, a surge of relief flooded through Ailene. As the night had inched by, she had been so sure they had been on the brink of disaster. She had gotten herself in such a state, she had begun to second-guess her readings of the bones and even her dream.

All she had been able to think about was the 'Death Tide' and how she should have warned everyone. In the aftermath, she was thankful that she had trusted her instincts—however, she never wanted to pass a night like that again.

"Are you well?"

Ailene glanced back to find Muin watching her. "Of course," she replied quickly.

"A shadow just passed across your face," he observed.

Ailene let out a nervous laugh. Muin knew her better than anyone; he had always been able to read her expressions easier that most folk. "I'm just weary," she said, deliberately breaking eye contact with him, "and relieved that the siege was a success."

She glanced up to see Muin still observing her. His lips parted to speak, but movement to his right, at the entrance to the broch, caught his eye.

A brown haired and bearded warrior, sweat-soaked and wild-eyed, rushed in.

"Mungo." Muin put down his cup and rose to his feet. "What are you doing here?"

Ailene went still. Mungo mac Muir had not come on this campaign with them. The Eagle warrior had remained behind with Talor and the others.

"Balintur," Mungo gasped the name as he strode across the floor toward them.

Ailene's meal curdled in her belly then. She knew what the warrior's next words would be, before he uttered them.

"The village is under attack."

Chapter Twenty-five

Smoke Over Balintur

Balintur
Territory of The Eagle

CATHAL MAC CALUM sat upon his pony at the brow of the hill, his gaze sweeping over the village that nestled into the valley below. Shouts rose into the still air. After days of howling winds, a morning of utter tranquility had dawned. The smoke rising from the roofs of the dwellings within the village rose vertically into a dull-grey sky.

"They'll break through the north gate soon, Da." Cathal tore his gaze from where his warriors boiled around the base of the high stone walls surrounding the village, to where his daughter sat. She rode a magnificent grey stallion. The beast was high-spirited and did not like being held back from battle. It danced now, tossing its head. However, Mor held the pony in check. "Tamhas brought the battering ram down with him."

"They'd better," Cathal rumbled. "I tire of waiting. It's now well past noon, and they still haven't managed to breach it ... maybe they should focus their attention on the south gate instead."

The siege had not started well. A deep ditch filled with iron spikes now ringed the walls, making it impossible to get close enough to scale them. Arrows rained down, thudding into the shields his warriors held aloft. However, one or two found their mark, bringing down the men and women laying siege to Balintur.

Cathal ground his teeth at the sight, and his stocky bay stallion—the pony he had taken from Tarl mac Muin a few months earlier—snorted and tossed its head in response.

Every warrior was precious—he wanted to lose as few as possible during the attack. Protect An Teanga or attack Balintur—Cathal had not taken long to make his decision. Much to his son's ire, he had taken Tormud mac Alec's advice.

"I'm not waiting much longer," he growled. Cathal hated to look on while others fought. He loved to be in the thick of the fighting, where he could hear the screams and breathe in the stench of battle.

However, Tormud and his son had convinced him to wait on the edge of the valley while they breached the walls. The plan had made sense—it still did—yet Cathal now seethed with impatience.

"Surely there can't be four hundred of them inside those walls." Beside him, Mor leaned forward in the saddle and peered down at the village.

Cathal frowned. He too had expected to see a number of them camped around the perimeter, yet the cottars working the fields outside the village had fled inside the moment the horn had wailed across the valley, warning the inhabitants of an imminent attack.

"It seems unlikely," he replied. "Perhaps they have moved some of their force north again?"

"Why would they do that?"

A deep scowl furrowed Cathal's brow as he pondered the question. "I don't know."

A moment later a hunting horn sounded, booming through the stillness of the early afternoon.

A grin stretched across Cathal's face, and he glanced over at Mor. "Finally! Come, lass. Let's go and spill some blood."

His daughter stared back at him, her moss-green eyes gleaming.

Without another word, they urged their ponies down the hill, bringing a tide of warriors on foot—bearing pikes, swords, and axes—with them.

"They've breached the north gate!"

Donnel mac Muin's face was grim as he strode into the round-house he shared with his wife and children. Eithni stood before a glowing fire pit, Eara clutching at her skirts. The sight of them there, unarmed and vulnerable, made fear kindle in the pit of his belly. He had to protect Eithni and Eara.

"The Warrior keep us," his wife whispered. "I thought we'd hold out longer."

"They have an iron-tipped battering ram," Donnel replied. "The gates are strong ... but not indestructible."

The sounds of shouting reached them then; panic raced through the village like wildfire.

Donnel cursed. "We can't stay here." He strode forward, scooped Eara up into his arms, and took Eithni by the hand. They exited the round-house and hurried up the narrow alleyway beyond.

"Donnel!" A familiar voice hailed him. He turned to see his elder brother, Tarl, stride up behind him, his wife Lucrezia at his side. Lucrezia had donned plaid breeches and a leather vest and carried a sword at her hip. Tarl's wife had trained as a warrior when she had first come to live with them many years earlier. Over the years, she had not needed to join the others in battle, but since they had abandoned Dun Ringill, she had been forced to pick up a sword once more.

"They're just three streets back now," Tarl said, his face hard, "and closing in fast."

"We're trapped." Eithni replied. She was trying to remain calm, yet Donnel could hear the panic creeping into her voice. "There's nowhere to hide."

"We need to get to the walls," Donnel replied, meeting his brother's eye. He saw his own anger and determination reflected in Tarl's gaze. "Right now, it's the safest place in Balintur."

Tarl nodded. "There's a ladder to the east wall close by. Follow me."

"Loose!" Talor bellowed. An instant later he too let his arrow fly. Perched high atop the wall, he and the other archers were attempting to slow the tide of Cruthini that now poured into Balintur through the north gate.

They had managed to bring down a few—but the sheer number of the attackers that now surged into the village was making their task near to impossible. They were close to being overrun.

My kin.

Fear arrowed through him at the thought of Eithni and Eara in peril, before he reassured himself. His father would protect them. Like him, Bonnie could protect herself. She was on the walls too, leading the defense of the south gate with strict instructions to remain there no matter the circumstances. He did not want his sister fighting down in the village, not unless all hope was lost.

"Loose!"

Once again, a volley of feather-fletched arrows shot down from the walls, peppering the sea of jostling rectangular-shaped shields below.

Talor scowled as his arrow embedded into leather and wood, but not flesh. They were too tightly packed for him to find his mark easily. Talor thought about Mungo then, his friend, who had ridden for help. He had sent the warrior, who was the fastest rider in the tribe, south as soon as the sentries on the wall had spied the approaching army. If the siege of An Teanga had gone as hoped, they would be able to ride to Balintur's aid.

Mungo should have reached An Teanga by now.

They could not hold this village alone, not against such a large force.

"Fire at will!"

Talor notched another arrow, drew it back against his cheek, and let it fly, bringing down a man directly below him. The warrior let out a wail and crumpled, only to be trampled by the Cruthini pushing in through the gate behind him.

Why didn't Ailene warn us?

She had foretold that dark times lay ahead for The Eagle. Was this it? Would this last stronghold of his people fall to The Serpent as well?

No.

He would not let this village fall. He would defend it with his last breath.

Talor shifted his attention from the gates to the nearest ladder against the walls. He spied two Serpent warriors scaling it.

Two arrows whistled through the air. One caught the first warrior—a brawny man with red-gold hair—in the shoulder. The second pierced a dark-haired woman through the ribs. Crying out, they both let go of the ladder and slid back to the ground.

Talor reached into his quiver to grasp another arrow, only to find it empty. Casting his bow and arrow aside, he drew his twin axes.

It was time to fight the enemy face-to-face.

Muin saw smoke rising to the north and knew that it was coming from Balintur.

The bastards have torched it.

He urged Feannag on, and despite that the pony had been traveling all afternoon at a swift canter, it flattened into a gallop.

We're too late.

As soon as Mungo had delivered the news, they had saddled their ponies and ridden from An Teanga without delay. However, Balintur lay some distance to the north.

The day was waning now, the light draining from the sky. They had ridden as fast as they could, but it would not be swiftly enough.

Dread settled like a boulder in Muin's belly. He thought of his friends and family in Balintur.

How many of them still lived?

Muin pushed the question aside, glancing at where Varar rode alongside him.

The animosities of the past between The Eagle and The Boar had truly been healed. Varar's presence here was proof of it.

Although he had only just won back his fort, Varar had not hesitated. The Boar chieftain had ridden out with them, as had Fina, and he had brought as many warriors as he could spare, leaving just a small number behind to defend An Teanga.

Galan had remained at the fort, as had Tea and Ailene. His father was still unconscious when Muin left. It was up to Galan's first-born to lead The Eagle into battle. However, this time it was not a siege they were conducting but a race to prevent a massacre.

Thundering up the last incline, Muin reached the brow of the hill and drew Feannag up.

Next to him, Varar let out an explosive curse.

Balintur was indeed burning. Flames leaped high in the air from the tightly-packed dwellings inside the walls. Screams and cries for help knifed the air. Figures on foot streamed out of the south gate, although there was also fighting going on there, as warriors chased them from the village and cut them down before they had gone a furlong from the gate.

Bile rose in Muin's throat. Sensing movement to his right, he swung his gaze to where his brother had just reined in his pony.

Aaron stared down at the massacre, the inferno. Black smoke poured up into the darkening sky. His blue eyes, so much like his mother's, stretched wide, and a nerve flickered under one eye.

The same horror he saw in his brother's face also pulsed through Muin.

An image flashed through his mind then, the memory of Ailene's face. He had just swung up onto Feannag's back at An Teanga when she had rushed across the stable yard toward him.

She had stared up at him, tears running down her face, her lovely eyes haunted. "This is my fault, Muin," she had gasped. "I am to blame."

"No, you aren't," he had countered, irritation spearing through him. He did not need Ailene's self-recrimination over things that were beyond her control—not now.

Ailene had not corrected him. Perhaps sensing that his thoughts were now elsewhere, she had only backed away, her face stricken.

The look on her face still troubled him as he gazed down upon Balintur. While they had been focused on An Teanga, the enemy had been making plans of their own. Ailene blamed herself for not being able to warn them—but how would she have known The Serpent would do this?

Shoving aside his misgivings, Muin drew his sword and raised it high.

"For our people!" His shout echoed across the hillside, rising above the din of battle below. This fight was not just for The Eagle, but for all those who had stood at their shoulder over the past months. Stag, Wolf, and Boar warriors were all down there, fighting for their lives.

"For our people!" The cries answered him, breaking like storm driven waves against rocks.

And then, in a roar of rage and thundering hooves, they descended upon Balintur.

Chapter Twenty-six
Defeat

TALOR RAISED HIS shield just in time to deflect the vicious pike aimed at his belly. Knocking the weapon aside with one of his axes, he sunk the other into his attacker's skull. The man fell twitching onto the wall.

Breathing hard, Talor stepped over his body and prepared himself to face the next warrior, a huge woman with wild brown hair and cold grey eyes. Talor flexed his fingers around the handles of his axes. His body was starting to protest, every muscle screaming for rest. Sweat poured off him, and his vision blurred. He had been fighting on the walls, had hardly moved a few feet beyond his original position near the gates.

One by one he faced them. It was fortunate for him that the walkway atop the wall was narrow, for he would have been quickly outnumbered otherwise.

As it was, the Cruthini all had to wait their turn as they tried to kill him.

Talor had just jammed his axe into another attacker's throat, and pushed the warrior off the wall onto the churning crowd below, when something caught his eye.

Heart pounding, Talor dragged his gaze from where three more huge Cruthini men were climbing the ladder, to where a small yet fierce woman fought for her life in the melee at the base of the wall.

Terror slammed into Talor, turning his sweat-soaked body cold.

Bonnie.

Blood splattered her naked limbs, and her long slender braids twirled around her as she attacked, feinted, and parried. Her pert face was hard, twisted into a rictus of killing rage that made pride swell within him.

However, that pride extinguished like a tender flame in a winter's draft when a huge man with wild auburn hair came at her.

Talor recognized the warrior instantly. A thin silver scar slashed over his left cheek, and he wielded a huge iron sword with deadly precision.

Cathal mac Calum bore down upon Bonnie, and all Talor could do was watch.

They began their dance, while the fighting continued to rage around them. Bonnie was fearless, and she fought with every ounce of skill that Talor, Muin, and Donnel had taught her.

But it would not be enough. Talor knew that.

With a roar, he lunged toward the ladder. He had to get down to her. He had to intervene.

However, he had three Cruthini warriors in his way.

Lowering himself over the edge of the wall, Talor kicked the first man in the face before slamming his booted foot down on the hand that grasped onto the ladder. The man cursed him, his sword stabbing upward and narrowly missing Talor's thigh. But one more well-aimed kick sent the man tumbling off the ladder.

And in that moment, Talor saw The Serpent chieftain cut his sister down.

Time slowed, and the din of battle receded.

All Talor could hear was his own cry; all he could see was the shock on Bonnie's face as that long iron blade ran her through. And then she crumpled.

Cathal mac Calum kicked her aside, yanked out his blade and turned, hacking his way through the melee toward the heart of the village.

Talor wanted to follow him, yet a huge man wielding a double-headed axe was almost upon him now. He could not reach his sister, nor could he avenge her.

The world closed around Talor mac Donnel, and for the first time in his life he tasted the bitter gall of defeat.

Cathal loved the chaos of battle. When he was amongst it, he forgot everything: his grief at losing Lena and Dunchadh faded, his anger at being forced to abandon the lands his people had farmed for decades dimmed.

All the mattered was dealing out death.

Cathal cut down a Stag warrior who rushed at him as he strode into the clearing in the middle of the village. The man collapsed against him, his big hands clutching at Cathal's throat. With a snarl, The Serpent chieftain shoved him aside and strode on.

Stopping in the heart of the clearing, Cathal let his gaze travel around the chaos that his people had caused. The buildings around him burned, including the large round-house that dominated the southern edge of the clearing.

Acrid smoke choked the air. It stung the back of Cathal's throat, yet he paid it little mind. A vicious smile stretched his face. Indeed, only half the number of warriors he had expected resided around Balintur. Once they breached the north gate, the sheer numbers of his own people had crushed the defenders.

Joy pulsed in his breast.

By nightfall this village would be his.

The entire southern territory of The Winged Isle would belong to The Serpent.

"Da!" A tall woman strode toward him through the smoke. Blood and grime streaked Mor's proud face, although her eyes were aflame. She bore a gash to her right arm. Blood trickled down over her wrist to where her hand gripped her sword. But she did not appear to notice.

As his daughter approached, Cathal stiffened. It was not battle fury but alarm he saw in her eyes.

"We're under attack," she announced.

Cathal's victory smile faded. "What?"

"A large company of warriors, many of them on ponies, have just hit us. Most of them are entering through the north gate." Mor broke off there, breathing hard as her tall frame vibrated with outrage. "They're butchering us. If we remain here, we'll be trapped."

Cathal stared at his daughter for a long moment. If she had just struck him across the face, he would have been less shocked.

He could not believe it. In just a few instants, everything had changed. Victory had been so close he had almost been able to touch it. Now bitterness flooded into his mouth.

Cathal snarled a curse and spat on the ground, glancing around him. Indeed, he could hear shouting and screams coming from the northern end of the village. "We need ponies."

Both he and Mor had dismounted soon after entering the village, as father and daughter preferred to fight on foot. However, without ponies, they would be run down by the enemy. The burning dwellings were their allies now, for the thick smoke would make it difficult for the rescue party to spot friend from foe.

Unslinging his hunting horn, Cathal blew hard.

The sound boomed across the village, cutting through the shouting and the crackle of devouring flames.

Cathal sounded the horn once more, fury pulsing through him now.

He had wondered where the rest of the enemy force had been. The fact that only half the defense he had expected was here had initially concerned him, but once the battle had begun, he had forgotten his worries.

The rest of the enemy had indeed left Balintur. Unfortunately, the dogs had been close enough to come to their people's aid.

Cathal tore the horn from his lips and turned to the tide of Cruthini who flooded into the clearing. "Fall back!" he boomed. "Make for the south gate!"

Cold anger hammered through Muin as he drove Feannag through the narrow dirt streets between the smoldering ruins of houses. Inside the walls of Balintur, the carnage was even worse than he had expected. Bodies of men, women, and children littered the streets, butchered when they tried to flee.

Muin headed toward the central clearing, and on the way, he cut down any Cruthini who crossed his path.

It had taken some time to fight their way into the village, as the majority of the enemy had amassed there. However, once they had broken through, The Serpent warriors realized they were outnumbered.

And then, once that hunting horn echoed through the valley, many of them had simply turned and fled. Some had tried to steal ponies in order to escape the village quicker.

A frenzied man with long braided red hair threw himself at Muin now and tried to wrestle him off his stallion. Muin kicked him in the face, drew his knife, and stabbed the warrior in the neck.

"They're running!" Varar, who had just ridden his stallion into the central clearing, twisted around to meet Muin's eye. "I'll see how many we can bring down ... you and the others make the village safe."

Next to Varar, Fina swept her gaze over the surrounding devastation. Her beautiful face looked carven from stone, such was her fury.

Muin gave a curt nod, swinging Feannag around while Varar and Fina thundered off in the direction of the south gate.

The last of the daylight was fading when Muin finally swung down from Feannag. The gelding was lathered, his sides heaving. Breathing hard himself, Muin leaned against the pony's sweat-slick shoulder and stroked his neck. "Brave, lad," he murmured. "You've a warrior's heart, indeed."

Leading the pony through the streets, Muin scanned the milling crowd of survivors for familiar faces. So far he had not seen any of his kin and only a handful of his friends.

Dread lodged in a hard lump in his throat, but he would not believe any of them had fallen. Not unless he saw it with his own eyes.

Halfway along the street he met up with Aaron. His younger brother had found Donnel, Eithni, and Eara.

Relief made Muin's heart pound as he embraced them. Donnel was limping, his face splattered with blood. Eithni's face was bloodless, and Eara clung to her leg, weeping.

"Have you seen Bonnie or Talor," Donnel asked. His uncle's grey eyes were clouded with worry. "I haven't glimpsed either of them since before the battle began."

Muin shook his head. "I haven't checked around the north gate yet. Let's go."

Facing the carnage at the gate required a strong stomach. Bodies were piled three high in places where the fighting had been at its most intense. Many of the Cruthini corpses bore fletched arrows from the archers.

Muin craned his neck up at the wall. There was not a soul there now, but he knew that since his cousin had some skill with a bow, he would have been up there at some point, defending the gate.

Moving through the dead, Muin's mouth gradually flattened into a hard line.

So much carnage, so much blood. It all seemed so pointless. Cathal mac Calum had brought his people to a new land only to bring them to their doom. Was it really worth all this to him?

Eithni's cry brought Muin up short.

He swiveled to see his aunt pry Eara off her leg, pick up her skirts, and sprint over to where a ladder lay against the north wall.

Muin's gaze followed her, and his breathing hitched.

Talor sat propped up against the base of the ladder, head bowed. Bonnie lay in his arms.

Chapter Twenty-seven
Burying the Dead

CATHAL FLATTENED HIMSELF against the pony's neck as arrows flew overhead. The beast, which he had stolen from a Wolf warrior he killed, bolted south in panic. Cathal did not care that he had lost control of the mare. The sooner it got him away from those in pursuit, the better.

Many of his people had escaped Balintur, although it was only through ruthlessness they had managed it. They had fought their way out of the village like cornered wolves, escaping through the ruins of the south gate.

Mounted warriors had come after them, hounding them south.

It was only when Cathal and his followers were many furlongs from the village that their pursuers eventually abandoned the chase. And when Cathal managed to pull up his pony and look around at his companions, a wave of chilling nausea swept over him. Night had fallen. A slender sickle moon had risen, casting a silvery light over the company, highlighting just how few remained.

Four hundred had ridden into Balintur.

There looked to be fewer than a hundred of his warriors left now.

Next to Cathal, Artair sagged against his horse's neck. His brother had taken a wound to the chest as they thundered out of Balintur. His face now twisted in agony, yet he had not uttered a noise during the journey south.

Mor rode up to Cathal. She was bleeding from her right shoulder, where an enemy hand axe had grazed her. Her wild auburn hair was tangled and sweat-soaked, and she swayed slightly upon the dun pony she too had wrested from one of the enemy. Tormud urged his pony up behind her. His weathered face was thunderous, his dark eyes blazing.

Cathal swallowed bile. How had this happened? It was supposed to have been a glorious victory, the moment when The Serpent would finally gain the upper hand over the united tribes of this isle. Instead, it had all soured.

"Cathal! Cathal!" A man's voice called out. "Where is the chieftain?"

"I'm here," Cathal snarled. "What is it?"

A man rode through the knot of ponies and men and women who had traveled on foot behind them. There were few warriors on foot, for the enemy had run most of them down. The newcomer had ridden in from the south, and although his face was strained, he was not sweat-soaked and bloodied like those surrounding him.

As he neared, Cathal recognized the man. His name was Aonghus, and Cathal had left him in charge of the defense of Dun Ringill in his absence.

"News has arrived from An Teanga," Aonghus informed him, his gaze darting around the grim faces of the surrounding warriors. He could sense that they had just run from a crushing defeat, although like Cathal, the warrior could hardly believe this had happened. It clearly distracted him from the message he had ridden hard to deliver.

"And?" Cathal growled.

Aonghus's gaze snapped to his chieftain, and his throat bobbed. "It has fallen. Yesterday ... a force that equaled that of the fort attacked and have taken it back."

Cathal went still, and suddenly everything fell into place. That was why Balintur had been missing so many folk, and why such a large group of armed warriors had descended upon them. They had just finished taking back An Teanga before riding north to defend their people.

Anger pulsed in Cathal's breast. He did not trust himself to speak. Tamhas had spoken true—they should have focused their attention upon protecting The Boar stronghold.

Long moments passed, and then The Serpent chieftain's attention shifted back to his daughter. He saw then that her cheeks were wet. Her eyes glittered. Behind her, Tormud's face sagged with exhaustion. Next to Cathal, Artair let out a soft groan of agony.

The Reaper's fingertips trailed down Cathal's spine, and he suppressed a shiver. It occurred to him then that he had not seen his son since he had sent him down to breach Balintur's north gate.

"Where's Tamhas?" he asked, his hoarse voice cutting through the night.

Only silence answered him.

A rain squall swept over the hillside, drenching Ailene. Bent low over Eòrna's neck, she rode down the last slope toward Balintur. A charred, ruined settlement greeted her; only the great wall surrounding the village seemed untouched, although even that was blackened in places where the fire had attempted to consume it.

Tears ran down Ailene's face, mingling with the rain.

She had been dreading returning here, dreading what she would find.

A rider had arrived at An Teanga from Balintur with the dawn, with news of what had happened. The Serpent had been driven out, but the cost was still too high. Many had fallen during the siege of Balintur, and the village was nearly destroyed by fire.

Behind her, she heard Tea mutter a soft oath. Tea and Galan had ridden north with her. The Eagle chieftain was not really strong enough to travel, yet he had insisted. Galan had said little during the journey, although whenever Ailene had glanced his way, she noted that his face was pale and strained.

He was stubborn to a fault. Not so different from his first-born son.

Anxiety fluttered in Ailene's belly then. She knew that Muin lived, although the messenger had brought news of many deaths among those she knew and loved.

Including Bonnie.

Ailene's vision blurred. The lass had been so young, so brave. Tears were gushing down her face now, and she could barely see. Scrubbing at them, she drew in a long shuddering breath.

She needed to regain self-control. A bandruí had to retain her serenity, even at times of tragedy. There would be much expected of her in the days to come.

They buried the dead in cairns on the hillside north of Balintur: rows of stone mounds that would change the silhouette of the hill forever.

So many had fallen that it was impossible to sing a lament for each individual. Instead, the kin and friends of the dead gathered before the cairns while Tea sang a haunting lament. It was a song that Tea's people, The Wolf, always sang for those they lost in harrowing circumstances.

Color drains from the sky
The winds of sadness blow
The red sun does not rise
The streams no longer flow.

The tide draws out forever
The stars dim and fade
Summer never comes
In eternal grief I wade.

After the last strains of Tea's voice faded, silence settled over the hillside. It was a chill morning. The sun was shining and the sky blue, yet a wintry wind tugged at the cloaks of the mourners as they huddled together before the cairns.

Ailene stood apart from it all, cloaked and hooded. She let silence lie for a while after Tea's lament, her gaze taking in the grieving faces of those surrounding her.

Donnel's handsome face appeared to have aged years since Bonnie's death. He stood, arms around his wife and youngest daughter, his grey eyes glittering with unshed tears. Eithni and Eara wept against him, while a few feet away stood Talor.

Her cousin's arm was in a sling this morning, his battered face wet as he wept. He had been injured and losing blood when they had found him, yet Eithni had tended to his wounds.

However, there were some wounds that the healer could not mend. And looking upon Talor, Ailene saw that his eyes were full of pain. It hurt her to look upon him. Once again, guilt cramped her belly.

Feeling someone's gaze upon her, Ailene shifted her attention to where a tall, broad-shouldered figure stood behind Talor. Muin. He did not touch him, for the grief that pulsed from Talor was a volatile, brittle thing. Yet Muin's strong, steadying presence filtered over his cousin nonetheless.

Ailene and Muin's gazes met and held. She saw the concern in his eyes. Since her return to Balintur the day before, they had barely spoken. There had been so much to do; they had both been kept busy. Ailene had thrown herself into helping Eithni tend to the injured and had slept close to Eithni and Eara the night before, in the make-shift tent they had erected.

She had deliberately avoided Muin and knew it confused him. However, she needed to ready herself for facing the chieftains. She had to tell them about the 'Death Tide'—a confrontation she was not looking forward to.

You will find out soon enough why I've kept my distance, mo ghràdh.

My love. Aye, she loved Muin with a fierceness that frightened her. It was not the love for a brother or a friend, but something else, something that made it feel as if her heart had just been wrenched out of her chest.

Dragging her gaze from her lover, Ailene breathed in the scent of the dried herbs she was burning in the clay pot she held before her: juniper berries and pine needles to protect and purify this sacred spot.

It was now her role to complete the burial ritual.

Ailene moved along the line of cairns, leaving the scent of burning juniper and pine behind her. Despite the cold weather she was barefoot. It was important in these rituals for the bandruí to be in contact with the earth.

Passing each mound, Ailene whispered a blessing for each soul to find peace in the afterlife. And as she walked, the sounds of quiet sobbing from the mourners followed her.

Chapter Twenty-eight
This is My Fight

AILENE FINISHED SPEAKING and silence fell in the tent.

Forcing herself not to stare down at her feet, Ailene kept her chin raised. However, her hands, clasped upon her lap, were clenched so hard together that they ached. On the other side of the fire, the four chieftains of the united tribes stared back at her.

None of them looked happy.

Galan's face had turned to stone, Varar's gaze had narrowed, Wid was scowling, and Tadhg's bearded jaw clenched.

Ailene drew in a slow, steadying breath.

She expected no different, and yet her pulse had started to race. Her attention shifted from the chieftains then, to where their kin flanked them. There were no friendly expressions there either. The likes of Eithni, Lucrezia, and Tea merely looked stunned, while both Talor and Muin's faces had paled.

"When exactly did you see the 'Death Tide'?" Galan asked, breaking the heavy silence.

Ailene met The Eagle chieftain's eye. "Just before you departed to take back An Teanga," she replied softly. "I wanted to cast the bones once more before the battle."

"And yet you never spoke of your findings to anyone?" Varar asked. His voice was quiet, although edged with displeasure.

"You'd already changed your plans because of me," Ailene answered. "I didn't want you to call off the siege."

"What if it had ended in disaster?" Galan asked. His tone was as inscrutable as his face. His lack of emotion made Ailene's nervousness increase.

"I realized my mistake as soon as you all left," she admitted. She had walked into this meeting planning to speak the truth. She would not lie or make excuses for herself. They would know she had erred, and that she was sorry for it. "I spent the whole night pacing the camp in dread ... I was so sure I'd made a terrible mistake." She broke off there, stealing a glance in Muin's direction. Like his father, Muin's expression was impossible to read. "When the riders arrived from An Teanga, I felt as if I'd just had a knife removed from my throat. My earlier prediction had come true ... it had been the right thing to take back An Teanga."

"But at great cost," Tadhg mac Fortrenn rumbled. "Drawing such a large number of our strength away from Balintur made us vulnerable to attack. This is exactly what I feared."

"You think The Serpent got wind of our campaign to An Teanga?" Varar raised a dark eyebrow. "And decided to seize the opportunity to attack?"

The Stag chieftain shrugged his broad shoulders in response. "Whatever the reason, they laid siege to Balintur while you were gone ... and if you hadn't arrived when you did, the rest of us would have perished." Tadhg paused here, his blue eyes narrowing. "Cathal mac Calum hit us with his full force. He came for a massacre ... and that's what he nearly achieved."

Silence fell, tension rippling through the large, cone-roofed tent.

"The 'Death Tide' was indeed a warning of this." Ailene spoke up, voicing what she knew all present were thinking. "But the bones did not give me any idea of when or where it would happen."

"But that doesn't mean you should have kept your mouth shut," Wid mac Manus's accusing voice cut through the tent. His dark brows had knitted together, and his cheeks had flushed. Ailene had seen Wid often over the years, but she had rarely witnessed him angry like this. "We've all lost many good warriors. You very nearly doomed everyone."

Ailene's spine stiffened, anger surging. "Punish me for withholding omens if you wish, but don't hang the fate of us all around my neck," she said coldly. "I have only ever tried to do what is best for our people."

No one spoke. However, Ailene continued to stare back at Wid, daring him to challenge her again. The Wolf chieftain's face turned thunderous.

Tension rippled through the tent. Eventually, Galan broke it. "Leave us now, Ailene." His voice was gentle although the lines of his face made him look severe. "We must discuss what you have told us."

And we must decide your fate.

Queasiness intruded, penetrating the anger that pulsed within Ailene. She nodded, dropping her gaze. Of course they would not want her present while they argued over what to do with her. She had no idea what the punishment was for bandruís who withheld omens from their people.

Was it banishment ... or stoning?

She could feel Muin's gaze boring into her, yet she did not look his way. She was too angry to meet anyone's eye now. She just wanted to be far from all these accusing stares.

Turning from the fire and the ring of faces still watching her, Ailene walked from the tent.

Outdoors, the afternoon was still cold and breezy. A pale blue sky and watery sun looked down upon her. Fluffy clouds raced across the heavens. She stood in the center of Balintur. The meeting tent had been erected in the clearing, next to the charred ruin of the large roundhouse where the chieftains used to gather.

The rest of the village was deserted. Everyone lived outside the walls at the moment, in clusters of hide tents, while work began on rebuilding the huts. It was the worst time of year for this to have happened. It was now a moon till Mid-Winter Fire. Although most of the food stores had survived the attack, they had little time to rebuild the village before the snows came.

Ailene strode through the village to the north gate, fury still churning within her. She knew she had made a mistake, but Wid had glared at her as if she had personally wielded the blade that had cut the folk of Balintur down.

They wanted to turn her into a scapegoat.

Drawing her fur cloak about her, she passed through the gate and into the make-shift settlement beyond. However, she was in no mood for company, so she took the dirt track north that led up to where the row of fresh cairns stood out against the blue sky.

Ailene's throat constricted although no tears welled at the sight of the tombs.

The situation was too serious to weep over. She felt brittle, as if the wind that buffeted her as she walked was blowing right through her.

Ailene was so deep in thought, so agitated, that she did not notice the tattoo of approaching hoof beats at first. It was only when the ground beneath her bare feet trembled that she realized a pony was approaching fast behind her.

Jumping back off the track, Ailene spun around to see who was in such a hurry.

Muin, astride Feannag, bore down on her.

The severe expression on his face, so similar to the one she had seen upon his father's, made Ailene's breathing catch. Did he hate her now, and had he come after her to tell her so?

Reaching Ailene, Muin drew his stallion up alongside.

Then he leaned toward her, one strong arm encircling her back. An instant later he lifted Ailene up onto the pony's back so that she perched in front of him.

Ailene gasped. "What are you doing?"

Muin did not reply. Instead, he urged Feannag into a fast canter and they took off up the hill, heading north.

Perched upon the pony's withers, Ailene had no choice but to cling to Muin or risk toppling off.

But still, Muin did not utter a word. His big body was rigid; she could feel the tension pulsing through him.

On they raced, leaving Balintur behind. Once the village was out of sight, Muin angled his pony north-east toward the oak woods a few furlongs distant, where Ailene had spent so many afternoons collecting herbs. Dread shivered through her when Muin slowed his pony, and they crunched through a carpet of dead leaves.

It was sheltered in the woods. The oaks kept the biting wind at bay. Tall trunks and a canopy of naked branches surrounded them. It suddenly seemed very quiet in here, with not even the twitter of birdsong to break the tense hush.

"Why have you brought me here?" Ailene finally asked. She was aware her voice was shrill, but she could not help it. She tensed, readying herself for another attack.

"I had to get you out of Balintur," Muin replied; his voice had a harsh edge to it. "Things became heated between the chieftains after you left. I won't have any of them hurt you."

Ailene's breathing hitched. "So, you don't share Wid's view?"

Muin growled a curse. "Of course not."

Ailene pulled away from him, craning her neck around so she could see his face. Muin's expression was stony, his grey eyes narrowed. With a jolt, she realized he was as angry as she was.

"I admit I was at fault," she said, her voice low. "I should have told you all about the 'Death Tide'."

"Aye." The word came out in a growl. "But even if you had, it wouldn't have stopped the attack. It was too late

... and how would any of us have known what was going to happen?"

Ailene opened her mouth to answer, but Muin pushed on, cutting her off. "If you'd told us, and we'd called off the siege of An Teanga, that fort would still belong to The Serpent ... and Balintur would have been attacked all the same."

Ailene stared at him, taken aback by his vehemence.

"I'm not going to let them blame you for the massacre," Muin continued. "They can discuss matters all they like ... but no one is going to lay a hand on you. I'll kill anyone who tries."

The tone of voice Muin used then, flint-hard, left Ailene in no doubt that he meant his words.

"Do they want to punish me?" she asked finally. Despite her brave face, fear fluttered up inside her.

He nodded. "Tadhg and Wid especially are furious ... they lost many warriors in the attack. "Da and Varar are trying to convince them to show you mercy."

"Varar?"

Muin grunted. "Aye ... I'm as surprised as you."

They had reached the heart of the woodland now, and the press of trees and undergrowth had become too dense for them to continue riding. Muin swung down from Feannag before helping Ailene to the ground.

Face to face now, Ailene felt heat creep up her neck. Muin's gaze was so intense it robbed her of the ability to breathe, to think. With a great effort she rallied her thoughts and straightened her spine.

"This is my fight, not yours, Muin," she said firmly. "You can't go against the chieftains. I won't let you put your life at risk. The folk of this isle make enemies for life. One day you'll be chieftain of The Eagle ... you can't sour your relationships over me."

Muin took a step closer to her. He was standing so near that Ailene had to raise her chin to keep holding his eye. "I'd set this isle alight for you," he said gruffly. "I'd make every man on this rock my mortal enemy if it saved you."

And with that he hauled her into his arms, his mouth covering hers.

Chapter Twenty-nine
A Good Man

IT WAS A hungry, dominant kiss—one edged with a desperation Ailene had never sensed in Muin. He was afraid for her, she realized with a jolt.

His hands were all over Ailene then, possessing her. They slid down the column of her back and cupped over her buttocks. Muin then pulled her hard against him, grinding their hips together as the kiss deepened.

Ailene's head swam, her senses reeling. She had never been kissed like this; it was as if he wanted to devour her. Heat pulsed between her thighs, and she let out a low whimper. Hunger rose within her, deep and fierce. Ailene locked her arms around Muin's neck and kissed him back with equal violence.

In response, Muin lifted her up, so that her legs wrapped around his hips. And then he carried her over to the nearest oak. Ailene's cloak slipped from her shoulders. Muin kicked it aside, pushing her up against the trunk.

Their mouths locked once more as they savaged each other. And as their tongues tangled, Ailene fumbled with the laces on Muin's breeches, while he hiked her skirt up.

Freeing his shaft, Ailene wrapped her fingers around its solid heat. Her breath caught; he was so big, so powerful. She ached for him to be inside her.

With a growl, Muin grabbed her wrists. He lifted them high above her head and pinned them against the trunk before kneeing Ailene's trembling thighs apart and driving into her in one deep thrust.

The sensation of being deep inside Ailene made Muin's heart pound against his ribs with such force his head spun. He was buried to the root inside her, wrapped in her tight heat, and it was nearly driving him mad.

If the Gods struck him dead right now, then he would die a happy man.

Still holding Ailene's wrists pinned above her head with one hand, he started to move inside her, in slow, deliberate strokes that he knew would unravel her self-control.

Moments later Ailene started to cry out, high mewing sounds that made excitement ignite in his veins. Muin ground his hips against hers with each thrust, and her cries lengthened into a long keen of pleasure. She cried his name and arched up, her breasts thrusting toward him.

Releasing Ailene's wrists, Muin reached down and unlaced her vest. Underneath she wore a thin sleeveless tunic that left little to the imagination. Her glorious breasts, soft and high with small pink nipples, rose toward him with each shuddering breath. Muin continued his slow thrusts, while he bent his head and suckled each breast through the fine linen.

Ailene gasped and groaned, writhing against him. Her hands tangled in his hair, pushing him against her breasts, demanding more.

Pleasure pulsed through Muin's groin, building in intensity with each thrust. He could feel his stomach muscles tightening in anticipation, yet he held himself back. He loved seeing Ailene like this.

She was an incredible woman. Sensitive, wise, and brave. He would not let the others blame this tragedy on her.

He would make her forget all the sadness, all the grief. He wanted to lose himself in her and forget his own loss. The Reaper had cast a long shadow over them all, yet in the midst of grief and pain, there was also love and life.

He took Ailene now to remind them both of that fact.

She writhed against him then, her lush body shuddering as she found her release, but still Muin did not cease driving into her. She was pleading with him now, and he could feel the heat and wetness of her core as he slid deep once more.

It was slowly unraveling him.

Yet he did not increase his pace. Instead he let trembling wrack Ailene's body, let her sob with pleasure, and only then did he give himself up to her, thrusting into her with a frenzy that made it hard to breathe.

The small fire crackled in the darkness, sending up a spray of sparks when Muin added a handful of sticks to it.

Pressed up against the wall of his chest, Muin's fur mantle covering them both, Ailene relaxed properly for the first time in days. A feeling of safety crept over her, suffusing her limbs with a warmth that had nothing to do with the hearth that burned before her.

"Are you hungry?" Muin asked, his breath feathering against her ear.

Ailene grimaced. In the aftermath of their lovemaking, her appetite, which had been non-existent over the past days, had returned, leaving her belly aching and hollow. "Starving," she admitted.

"I didn't have time to gather much." Muin reached left, digging into a leather satchel. "But I managed to pack some bread and cheese."

He might as well have told her he had brought a great feast with him. Ailene's mouth filled with saliva at this news.

She eagerly took the hunk of bread and wedge of sharp cheese he passed her, taking a large bite. The bread was very heavy, filled with crushed oats and barley, yet it was fresh.

"This is delicious," she mumbled through her next mouthful. "Where did you get it?"

"Ma had left a few loaves cooling before the meeting ... so I helped myself to one."

Ailene twisted her head, to see that Muin's mouth had lifted at the edges. The sight of his strong face, and the tenderness in those storm-grey eyes, made her throat thicken. "I'm glad you came after me," she murmured. "I was too angry to be left alone with my own thoughts."

He huffed. "You can always talk to me, Ally. You always could."

Ailene swallowed a mouthful of bread and cheese. "I know," she whispered.

They both fell silent then, each retreating into their own thoughts.

Ailene finished her bread and cheese before brushing crumbs off the fur mantle wrapped around them. It was a cold, breezy night, although the surrounding trees kept the wind off them. Ailene curled against Muin's chest, enjoying the heat of the fire. She wished they could stay there forever, that all the sadness and hardship their people had endured over the past months could cease to exist.

But she knew this night was merely a reprieve from the rest of the world. She could not hide from it forever.

"You know I'm going to have to go back there," she said finally.

Muin's body stiffened against hers, and she sensed him readying himself to argue with her.

"You want to protect me," she continued, before he could speak. "But you can't shelter me from this." She reached down then and took his hand, interlacing her fingers with his. "There are some things that I must face alone."

"I won't let them harm you," Muin replied. His voice held a rough edge, his expression hardening. "I won't let them take out their grief and rage on a woman who has only tried to help them."

Ailene released a slow breath, squeezing her eyes shut. "Then I'm grateful you will be at my side tomorrow." She paused then, a shiver passing through her as she considered the future. "However, they may decide to banish me."

"Then I will go with you."

Ailene's eyes flew open. She pulled away from Muin, meeting his gaze fully. "You can't do that."

His jaw was set as he stared back at her, a stubborn light in his eyes. "I can."

"But you're Galan's first-born … you're destined to lead The Eagle one day."

He shook his head. "I'm destined for whatever life I choose. I'll not have my fate dictated by others. If they cast you out, I'm going with you. I have no wish to remain with my people if you cannot."

Ailene's throat tightened. "You'd give everything up?" she whispered. "For me?"

Muin's mouth quirked. "Aye … without question." He reached up then, raking a hand through his hair. "The responsibility for our tribe has never sat easily upon my father's shoulders. Peace is all he has ever wanted, and yet it has eluded him. He even wed a woman from an enemy tribe in an attempt to build another future for us all."

"Aye, but that ended well for him."

"It could have easily been different … he could have ended up unhappily wed to my mother," Muin replied. "My father's a good man, but I don't want his life."

Ailene reached out and traced the line of his strong jaw, feeling the rasp of stubble under her fingertips. "*You* are a good man, Muin mac Galan." Her voice was low, husky. "The best I've ever known. You have a big heart, and I love you."

She watched his pupils dilate, before his mouth stretched into a full smile. "I've always loved you, Ally," he said softly. "There has only ever been one woman for me ... and there only ever will be."

Chapter Thirty
Meeting with the Chieftains

THEY RODE BACK into Balintur just after dawn. Smoke rose from the clusters of tents outside the village walls, merging with a mantle of low cloud that had settled over the valley. The burned-out shell of the settlement below was an eerie sight, a reminder of just how far people were prepared to go for power. Ailene's brow furrowed at the sight of it.

Cathal mac Calum would now be ruing the day he ever set foot upon this isle.

Folk noticed their approach, and as they neared the first tents, a tall dark-haired woman stepped out to greet them.

Tea.

"I'm glad you came back." The Eagle chieftain's wife's gaze swept over them. Indeed, Ailene saw relief in her eyes, although her expression was guarded.

Seated behind Muin this morning, her arms wrapped around his waist, Ailene felt her lover tense. He had agreed to return to Balintur with her, yet he was not happy about it.

"I'd like to speak to the chieftains," Ailene called out.

Tea nodded, her expression turning resigned now. She had expected this. "They will find you in the meeting tent shortly. Go on ahead."

Muin and Ailene rode into the deserted village, Feannag plodding through the soot-blackened paths leading to where a large hide tent rose up amongst the ruins.

"How long will it take to rebuild the village?" Ailene asked Muin as she took in the devastation.

"A couple of moons," Muin replied, his voice a low rumble. Unlike that morning, when they had lain curled together by the fireside, his body was rigid against hers, each nerve on alert. "They torched every last dwelling."

Reining the pony up outside the tent, Muin dismounted before helping Ailene down.

She turned to Muin, noting the strain on his face.

"Remember what I said last night," he said, stepping toward Ailene and brushing a lock of stray hair from her face. "If any of them tries to harm you, I won't be held responsible for my actions."

Fear fluttered in Ailene's belly at this proclamation. Once again she did not doubt him. Muin never made vows he did not mean. However, the thought of him trying to defend her against warriors who were his equal in combat made her feel queasy.

She could not let him do that.

If it came to pass, she would not.

Stepping close to Muin, she reached up and cupped his face with her hands. "Your support means a lot to me, my love," she murmured, holding his gaze steadily. "But this is my battle, not yours. Whatever happens, please remember that."

A lump of peat burned in the fire pit in the center of the tent, glowing gold. Ailene stared at it, forcing down nervousness.

The four chieftains had arrived, bringing their closest kin with them. Galan had brought not just Tea and Aaron, but his two brothers and their offspring. It seemed this morning's meeting was to have an audience.

However, despite that Donnel and Talor were in attendance, Eithni and Eara were absent.

Ailene glanced up briefly when Talor entered, although her cousin did not look her way. His face, which was usually relaxed, was stone-hewn this morning.

Does he blame me for Bonnie's death?

Ailene's belly contracted, nausea rising. She had been relatively calm earlier, yet now that the chieftains were before her, it felt as if a tribe of brownies were trying to twist her gut in knots.

Drawing in a deep breath, and then another, Ailene raised her chin and surveyed them.

Next to her, she felt Muin's solid presence. He sat close, so that their thighs brushed. The heat of his body enveloped her, giving her strength. She did not need to glance his way to know that he was glowering across the fire pit at the four men he was ready to see as his enemies.

None of the chieftains were smiling.

Both Galan and Varar were as difficult to read as ever, their faces carefully composed masks. However, beside Varar, Fina was scowling. She kept shooting her husband warning looks, which he was making a point of ignoring.

Wid sat immovable and silent, his bearded face hard, while next to him, deep grooves furrowed Tadhg's heavy brow.

They did not look any more welcoming than they had the day before.

Fear rose within Ailene, and her breathing quickened. She had hoped that a night to think on things would have made these men soften toward her; yet it seemed reflection had only made The Wolf and Stag chieftains more hostile.

Silence drew out in the tent, and finally unable to bear the tension any longer, Ailene cleared her throat. "Have you made your decision about my fate?"

"Aye," Varar replied. He spoke softly, although the tone of his voice gave nothing away. "We discussed matters at length last night."

The Boar chieftain paused here. Beside her, Muin shifted, his thigh pressing hard against hers. Resisting the urge to reach out and take her lover's hand, Ailene held Varar's stare.

"You made a mistake," Varar continued, "but it was an honest one." His gaze shifted from her then, flicking to where Wid and Tadhg sat as silent and still as boulders. "In our anger and grief, we have overlooked the good advice that you have given us over the past months." His attention flicked back to Ailene. "You have not steered any of us wrong. You predicted The Boar and Eagle would be united in marriage and that it was the right time to take back An Teanga ... and both those things have come to pass. You also rode after our army when you had a vision of disaster. We changed our plans because of you." Varar broke off here, his handsome face tightening. "You also warned us that dark times lay ahead for The Eagle. You might not have realized it at the time ... but the 'Death Tide' was linked to that portent."

"You are young and only just gaining confidence in your abilities." Galan spoke up then. "Already you have been put through much more stress than Ruith ever was during her many years as bandruí. Varar's right ... your error was not made out of malice."

Silence fell in the tent.

Ailene stared at Galan. "You're not punishing me?" She did not want to ask the question, for she feared she had misunderstood him. However, she had to know. Her pulse started to throb in her ears while Muin's thigh kept its steady pressure against hers.

"No, we aren't," Galan replied, his face softening. "Enough darkness has fallen upon us all of late, without us turning on each other." He shot a pointed look across at The Wolf and Stag chieftains. Neither man had yet uttered a word. "So it's agreed then. We shall let this lie?"

It took a while for Wid and Tadhg to reply.

The Stag chieftain's wife, Erea, cast her husband a censorious look, nudging him in the ribs with her elbow.

"Aye," Tadhg grunted. "You are right. The lass made a mistake … who of us here hasn't?"

All gazes turned then to Wid. He wore a thunderous expression now. Unlike Tadhg's wife, Alana remained still and silent at his side and did not try to catch his eye. However, their surviving son, Calum, cast his father a questioning look, his dark brows knitting together.

"I don't like this," Wid finally replied, his voice a low growl, "but I see I am outnumbered."

Watching The Wolf chieftain, Ailene clenched her jaw. She knew Wid had been through much of late. He had not yet recovered from losing his youngest, Bred, in the Battle of Bodach's Throat. Before his son's death, Wid had been an even-tempered man who was quick to forgive and even quicker to laugh. But these days there was a bitter edge to him that had dug permanent lines into his face. Yet despite that she sympathized with him, Ailene did not appreciate the thinly veiled animosity he held toward her.

The other chieftains could see past their own grief, why could not he?

Holding Wid's gaze, Ailene drew in a deep breath. "Thank you, Wid," she murmured. "Please remember that we are all on the same side. I have only ever wanted to help our people."

The Wolf chieftain stared back at her, and she saw a shadow move in the depths of his dark blue eyes. "Aye," he rumbled. "I know, lass."

Ailene exited the tent on shaky legs.

Muin had stayed behind to join the discussion about the first stages of the rebuild of Balintur. However, she could leave.

Tilting her head to the overcast sky, Ailene whispered her thanks. She had not believed she would escape punishment. She wondered which of the chieftains had been instrumental in the decision—instinct told her it was Varar.

"There you are." Ailene turned to see that Fina had also left the tent. "I was hoping you hadn't gone far."

Her friend crossed to her and, linking arms, the pair walked toward the ruins of the north gate. Ailene cast Fina a glance, but she was not looking her way. Fina still wore her hair in fine braids, which she had pulled up into a high pony-tail; the style suited her, revealing her long neck and regal profile.

"Do I have you to thank for this?" Ailene asked.

Fina cut her a look, her gaze widening. "Why do you ask that?"

Ailene smiled. "You're a terrible liar. It's written all over your face. What did you say to Varar?"

Fina held her gaze a moment before favoring Ailene with an impish grin. "He wasn't hard to convince. I know the rest of you think Varar mac Urcal is a hard bastard, but that's just a shield. His heart is really as soft as porridge ... just don't ever tell him I said that."

Ailene laughed. The thought of Varar being soft-hearted was ridiculous, and yet she had witnessed how he had led the other chiefs inside that tent; Varar was the youngest of them, and had a blemished history with the other tribes, especially The Eagle. But Ailene would never forget how he had defended her.

Her smile faded then, when she remembered the grim look on some of the faces inside the tent. "Wid and Tadhg don't look happy about the decision though."

Fina shrugged. "But the peace holds between our tribes, that's all that matters. They will soften in time."

"And Talor? He hasn't been able to look me in the eye since I returned to Balintur."

Fina let out a sigh, her face clouding. "That's got nothing to do with you ... Talor blames himself for Bonnie's death. He keeps saying he should have gotten to her sooner."

Up ahead the north gate loomed, and the aroma of frying oatcakes wafted toward them.

"Did you know that it was Cathal mac Calum himself who slew Bonnie," Fina continued, her voice developing a hard edge. "She did well to hold out as long as she did."

A lump rose in Ailene's throat. She remembered Bonnie's bright hazel eyes, her quick smile, and even quicker wit. It was such a waste. "Bonnie's death wasn't Talor's fault," Ailene murmured.

"Just as the attack on Balintur wasn't yours," Fina reminded her firmly. "As Varar said back there … it's because of your warning that the siege of An Teanga was a success. Many of our people have fallen over the past few days, but The Boar territory has now been liberated and The Serpent is licking its wounds back in Dun Ringill." Fina's face and voice turned hard then. "Cathal mac Calum's days on this isle are numbered."

The two women walked in silence then, out of the ruined village and into the sea of tents that spread down the hillside beyond. Folk were out tending the fields already, the murmur of subdued voices lifting into the misty air.

"Varar and I will return to An Teanga tomorrow," Fina said, stopping and turning to Ailene. "We need to shore up the defenses, just in case the Cruthini get desperate."

Ailene nodded. It made sense. They had left a small number of warriors behind to defend the fort, but it was a temporary solution. "I will miss you," she said softly, meeting Fina's eye. "It will seem strange to live apart from each other."

Fina's full mouth curved. "I never thought I'd wed a Boar, let alone make An Teanga my home … but it goes to show that we never know what lies ahead. The Gods like to surprise us." Her smile turned sly then. "I'm glad to see you came to your senses regarding Muin."

Ailene's gaze widened. "Don't tell me you knew too?"

"I'd suspected something … I'd occasionally catch him watching you in a way that warned me his feelings went far deeper than friendship. I was disappointed when he admitted to me that you didn't want him."

Ailene ran a hand down her face. "Luckily, I realized what I stood to lose before it was too late."

Fina grinned. "So, you love my hulking cousin, then?"

"Aye … to distraction."

Chapter Thirty-one
The Path of Vengeance

"I GIVE YOU my thanks, Varar."

The Boar chieftain turned, surprise filtering across his face. Muin had waited till the others had left the tent. He and Varar had been the last to depart when Muin had spoken.

"No thanks are needed," Varar replied with a half-smile. "Fina would have gelded me if I'd let Ailene be punished ... plus the seer wasn't going down without a fight." His expression grew serious then. "Instead, I owe the lass *my* thanks."

The sincerity in the man's tone took Muin aback. He had not held a high opinion of Varar mac Urcal once. Like the rest of his kin, he had been suspicious of him when he had arrived at the Lochans of the Fair Folk mouthing words of peace.

And yet, Varar had been true to his word.

The two men left the tent together, but Muin walked alone back to the encampment outside the walls. There, he found Ailene sharing a morning meal of oatcakes, butter, and honey with Tea, Fina, and Lucrezia. He joined them and ate his fill before leaving the women to talk.

Usually, Eithni would be with them—she and Tea spent most of their days together—but since they had buried Bonnie, the healer had kept largely to herself.

He found Eithni sitting by the fire pit in her tent, staring blankly at the flames. She glanced up when Muin entered and attempted a smile. However, the expression was strained. Her eyes remained haunted.

"I'm not intruding, am I?" Muin asked, hovering at the entrance.

Eithni shook her head. "I could do with the company ... sitting alone with my own thoughts is turning me maudlin."

"Where are the others?"

"Donnel has taken Eara down to the water to fish for flounder ... he wanted to distract her."

Muin smiled at this news, although the expression was tinged with sadness. Bonnie had loved to go spear fishing with her father.

"And Talor ... have you seen him?"

A shadow passed over Eithni's heart-shaped face. She shook her head. "I worry about him, Muin. He's barely spoken a word to any of us since the attack."

"I will talk to him ... if you think it will help?"

Eithni nodded. "Thank you." She motioned to a stool opposite. "Take a seat."

Muin did as bid, lowering himself onto the low stool and warming his hands over the fire.

"I'm sorry I didn't come to the meeting earlier," Eithni said after a brief pause. "But Donnel tells me that all is well ... and I am pleased. Ailene has only ever wanted to do good." She attempted a wan smile then. "I am happy for you both."

Muin breathed in deeply in an attempt to ease the pain in the center of his chest. Eithni was a gentle-hearted woman. Even in the midst of her own grief, she found room to care about others. Over the past days she had tended the injured despite her loss. She was truly remarkable.

Silence fell between them then, and after a long pause, Eithni broke it. "I never really understood Bonnie, you know ... she could be wild and reckless."

The corners of Muin's mouth lifted. "Aye ... but that was also part of her charm."

"I've feared for her over the years," Eithni replied softly. "As I have feared for you all. I know a warrior's life can be a short one, yet I'm angry with the Gods all the same for taking her from me."

"Is there anything I can do to help?" Muin asked, leaning forward. "I hate to see those I love in such pain. I feel so useless."

Eithni smiled then, and this time it did warm her eyes, for they crinkled at the corners. "You are far from useless. We are all lucky to have you in our lives," she replied, wiping her damp eyes. "Your strength will help your cousin keep a steady course ... please seek Talor out and watch over him in the days to come. I worry what he might do."

Muin found his cousin at the cairns, standing alone by the small stacked-stone mound that was Bonnie's resting place.

Approaching slowly, Muin took in the rigid set of Talor's shoulders. He was dressed in a leather vest and breeches and wore no cloak, despite the chill morning.

Muin stopped to the right of his cousin, taking in his profile.

Talor stared at the entrance to his sister's tomb, his face stony. His eyes burned.

Grief swept over Muin as he watched him. He too had loved Bonnie. He had trained her in swordplay, smiling at her good-natured insults as she did her best to get under his guard. The lass had burned as bright as a Gateway fire. It was hard to believe that she was gone.

Together, the two men stood in silence. Muin did not speak; it was not his way. He had always been more comfortable with silence than Talor.

Eventually, Talor broke the silence between them. "I told Bonnie to stay on the walls," he murmured. His voice sounded like it belonged to someone else: low and raspy. "Why could she never do as she was told?"

Muin did not reply. He got the feeling he was not expected to. Talor simply wanted someone to listen to him.

"I was too slow," Talor continued. Muin grew still at the bleakness in his voice. He had never seen Talor like this; his cousin had always been so cocky and cheerful. But it was as if all hope had left him. "I tried to reach her, but there were too many Cruthini."

Talor broke off there, and Muin saw that tears now trickled down his cheeks. But still he did not look his way. The pain on Talor's face felt like a blade to Muin's heart. He wished he could do something to ease it.

"She looked tiny down there," Talor whispered. "She was so fierce, fighting warriors twice her size. But when Cathal went for her, I knew it was over."

A lump rose in Muin's throat. He could imagine the scene. He had seen Cathal mac Calum fight. The man struck fear into most of his opponents' hearts. As brave and skilled as Bonnie had been, she would never have lasted long against the warrior.

"She was still breathing when I reached her." Talor's words were barely audible now. His cousin bent his head, his shoulders shaking. "She stared up at me with pleading eyes. Her lips moved but no sound escaped ... and then ... I felt the life drain out of her."

"She was a brave lass," Muin rasped out the words, his own eyes stinging. "This shouldn't have been her time."

Talor angled his head toward him then. His sea-blue eyes were aflame. "Cathal will eat iron for this," he growled, "and I will personally feed it to him."

Muin held Talor's gaze. He knew it was only anger and grief talking, yet his cousin's vehemence concerned him. "Don't seek the path of vengeance, Talor," he said, deliberately keeping his voice low and soothing. "It'll only destroy you."

Talor's face went rigid. "Let it," he snarled. "As long as I bring that Serpent turd down with me."

With that, Talor spun on his heel and strode away.

Muin let him go. Talor was too angry to argue with. He would only lose his temper if Muin tried to talk to him again. It was better to let him be, let the rage burn out of him.

Even so, misgiving feathered down Muin's spine as he watched Talor storm off. Although close, they were very different men. Muin had always felt boring and predictable next to his hot-headed, charming cousin. Once they had reached manhood, Talor attracted women to him with ease, whereas there had only ever been one woman Muin had ever wanted. Talor enjoyed female attention, even deliberately going after unavailable women over the years. He liked the chase as much as the capture. Muin was too straight-forward to enjoy such complications.

Once again, his focus had been wholly on Ailene.

There was a reckless side to Talor that Muin had never understood. He, like all in Dun Ringill, had heard the tale of how bitter and angry Talor's father, Donnel, had become after losing his first wife. His uncle raged at the world for a long while afterward. Only Eithni had been able to heal him.

Turning back to the cairns, Muin wondered if Talor was about to set off down the same path—one that could potentially destroy him.

Muin remained at the cairns for a while longer. They were a peaceful place, for the dead did not chatter. In the valley below, the sounds of industry and voices rose and fell as work got underway to clear the debris from the village. Shortly, Muin would join them, but for a moment longer he lingered at the tombs.

"I thought I might find you here." A soft female voice intruded upon his introspection. An instant later a hand brushed against his.

Muin glanced left to see Ailene at his side. Smiling, he interlaced her fingers with his. "I followed Talor up here," he admitted, "but he's not in a sociable mood."

"I know ... I passed him on the way here. He looked right through me."

Muin drew Ailene close and wrapped an arm around her shoulders. "Don't take it personally ... he's filled with grief and looking for an outlet. I didn't say much to him, but my few words were enough to make him angry."

Ailene's arms fastened around Muin's torso. She leaned into him, and the stress and strain of the morning drained away, cloaking them both in a gentle cocoon of contentment.

"You're strong, Muin," she murmured against his chest. "Not just physically ... but inside where it really counts. You're my anchor, especially now when our world is in chaos. When I'm with you, I feel like I can face anything."

Muin's mouth quirked. He placed a kiss on the crown of her head, breathing in the scent of rosemary from her thick peat-brown hair. "You're my strength too," he murmured. "I can weather any storm life throws at me, if you're at my side."

Epilogue
Curious Things

Balintur
Territory of The Eagle

One month later ...

THE SNOW WAS falling, delicate flakes fluttering down from a colorless sky. Ailene stepped out of the hut and angled her face up to it. She closed her eyes a moment and let the first flakes settle on her skin.

It was nearing the eve of the 'Long Night'; Mid-Winter Fire had arrived and with it the first snow of the bitter season.

Drawing her cloak around her, Ailene made her way through the village toward the south wall, where Muin was taking his turn at watch. It was late afternoon and the light was low; night would settle early, especially now the snow had come.

As Ailene walked, she took in the signs of industry around her. They had done much in the last moon. Many of the dwellings inside the walls had been rebuilt; only a few folk still resided in tents, and those had now been moved inside the walls for safety, and protection from the biting wind that could blast this side of The Winged Isle at times.

The hut she now shared with Muin had been rebuilt. While her lover had been standing guard on the wall, she had decorated the interior of their dwelling with boughs of scented pine. She had also hung holly from the rafters. A rich venison stew, which she would serve with oaten dumplings, had been bubbling over the fire pit all day. The meal would end with a heavy cake made with oats and dried plums, dripping in honey and served with thickened cream.

A huge oaken log that Muin had dragged in the day before burned in the hearth. They would enjoy watching it smolder for the next twelve days, as it encouraged sunlight and warmth to return to the earth.

Ailene could not wait to see Muin's face when he returned to the hut; it looked like a forest dell and was filled with delicious aromas.

Passing through the central clearing that had a new meeting house at one edge, Ailene skirted around a huge, unlit pyre of oak branches. After dark they would light the fire and pass around cups of warmed mead as they watched it burn.

Ailene reached the ladder that led up to the south wall and climbed up.

The snow was falling more heavily now, a silent flutter of white that settled over the surrounding hills. Spying Muin up ahead, Ailene waved to him.

He grinned as she approached. "Is that drualus in your hair?"

Ailene reached up and patted the sprays of green mistletoe that she had woven amongst her curls. "Aye, mo ghràdh," she said sweetly. "It is Mid-Winter Fire after all."

"You look beautiful," he replied, his grey eyes warm. "Especially with snowflakes dusting you like stars."

Ailene smiled at the compliment, stepping close and kissing him gently on the lips. "How much longer till your watch ends? I have a feast awaiting you back home."

"Not much longer," he assured her. "Talor should be here soon."

The good humor drained from his face then at the mention of his cousin. Ailene knew that he worried about Talor. They had all hoped his grief would lessen with the passing of time, yet he had become surly and solitary, often deliberately choosing shifts on the wall that would allow him to avoid spending time with friends and family. Even on nights like these.

Muin stepped closer to her. "Do you have your telling bones with you?" he asked.

"Aye ... why?"

"Can you cast them?"

Ailene raised her eyebrows. "What ... here in the snow?"

His mouth curved. "You haven't cast the bones in many days ... now is as good a time as any."

Ailene sighed. He was right. After the attack on Balintur, she had been wary of using her abilities as a seer. She was sometimes afraid of what the bones might tell her.

"I know you're nervous," Muin said softly, as if reading her thoughts, "but you mustn't shy away from your gift. Come ... cast the bones and tell me what you see."

"Very well." Ailene reached for the pouch at her waist. "But don't blame me if they bring ill tidings."

She poured the bones onto her palm, her fingers closing around them. Then she hunkered down and cast them at her feet. The telling bones clattered across the stone, coming to rest amongst the sprinkling of snowflakes.

Ailene's brow furrowed as she studied them.

"Well?" Muin asked when silence stretched out. He lowered himself down next to her, his gaze scanning the bones carven with the symbols of their people. "What do you see?"

"Curious things," Ailene replied. She glanced up, catching Muin's eye.

"No 'Death Tide' this time?"

"Thank The Hag no ... and no dark times ahead for The Eagle either."

Muin's gaze widened. "That's welcome news. What else?"

Ailene turned her attention back to the bones, leaning forward as she studied them more closely. The marks of the serpent, the eagle, and the selkie have fallen together," she said, "which hints that there will be a union between our two tribes."

"Between The Eagle and The Serpent?" Muin's voice was incredulous. "Are you sure?"

"I'm only telling you what I see." Ailene cast him a stern look. "Interpret what you will from it." She then leaned forward once more. "There's something else ... a sign I haven't seen in a long while."

Ailene reached out her hand, her fingertip tracing a line from where the sign of the rising moon sat above that of the cauldron. A smile stretched her face as realization settled. Finally, a reading of the bones that did not twist her belly into knots and make her break out into a cold sweat.

The Gods were capable of giving her good omens as well it seemed.

"What is it?" Muin asked, impatience creeping into his voice. Her silence was making him uneasy.

Still smiling, Ailene turned to him, cupped his face with her hands, and landed a stinging kiss upon his mouth. "Peace is coming to this isle," she announced.

Muin's eyes flew open wide in surprise, but Ailene was already reaching for her telling bones and scooping them up. "Come," she said, her smile widening to a grin of excitement. "We need to go and tell the others."

The End

From the author

I hope you enjoyed the second installment of THE PICT WARS.

WARRIOR'S SECRET was the first 'friends to lovers' tale that I've written, and I enjoyed exploring the development of their relationship. How do you go from seeing someone as 'just a friend' to being passionately in love with them? How do you deal with knowing that the love of your life doesn't feel the same way? I loved Muin's quiet strength, and Ailene's courage and sensitivity, and hope you did too!

As this book is set back in the mists of time, there were few historical events for me to anchor my story on. However, I have woven in a few cultural details I hope you appreciated.

In order to bring Ailene's role as seer to life, I had to do a bit of research into druidic practice back in ancient times.

Druids, both male and female, had important roles in ancient Celtic societies. I have two bandrui (female druids) in this tale. They did indeed divine the future in a number of ways: through visions, casting bones, or observing the flight or birds or formations of clouds. During the novel Ailene spends time in an oak forest. Oaks were a sacred tree for druids. In Pictish society, druids would have acted as priests, teachers, and judges. It was a role held in high esteem. Druids did not fight in battles, and spent their entire lives in training. They believed that the soul was immortal and passed on at death from one person to another.

The use of herbs was also important in druidic practice. For the ancient Druids, the healing and magical properties of herbs were inseparable from the larger cycles of the seasons, the movements of the planets, and the progression of human life.

Druids used herbs when creating rituals to celebrate festivals and significant life passages such as births, house blessings, weddings, funerals, and naming ceremonies. The ancient druids had nine 'sacred' herbs. They were henbane, mistletoe (drualus), vervain (verbena), clover, wolfbane (aconite), primrose, mint, mugwort, and anemone (Pulsatilla). Divining wands were often made of yew or ash.

Half way through the story, Ailene has an encounter with one of the 'Fair Folk' or the Aos Sí (literally 'people of the mounds') as they were also known. I thought it would add some richness to the story, especially given Ailene's role as seer. The Aos Sí were a fairy race in Irish and Scottish mythology. They are said to live underground in fairy mounds, across the western sea, or in an invisible world that coexists with the world of humans.

In ancient times, folk would appease the Aos Sí with offerings, and care was taken to avoid angering or insulting them. Often they are not named directly, but rather spoken of as "The Good Neighbors", or "The Fair Folk" (as in my stories), or simply "The Folk". The Aos Sí are generally described as stunningly beautiful, though they can also be terrible and hideous.

See you again soon, with another tale from the Dark Ages!

Jayne x

Historical and background notes
for WARRIOR'S SECRET

Glossary

Aos Sí or Fair Folk: fairies
bandruí: a female druid or seer
Broch: a tall, round, stone-built, hollow-walled Iron Age tower-house
Caesars: the Ancient Romans
mo ghràdh: my love

Place names

An t-Eilean Sgitheanach: Gaelic name for the Isle of Skye
Dun Ardtreck: a broch located on the Minginish Peninsula of Skye
Dun Ringill: an Iron Age hill fort on the Strathaird Peninsula of Skye
An Teanga: an Iron Age broch located on the southern coast of Skye
Dun Grianan: an Iron Age broch located on the north-western coast of Skye
Balintur: village in the north of The Eagle territory
The Black Cuillins: mountain range in the Isle of Skye

The four tribes of The Winged Isle*

The People of The Eagle (south-west)
The People of The Wolf (north-west)
The People of The Boar (south-east)
The People of The Stag (north-east)

Gods and Goddesses of The Winged Isle*

The Mother: Goddess of enlightenment and feminine energy—the bringer of change

The Warrior: God of battle, life and growth, of summer
The Maiden: Young goddess of nature and fertility
The Hag: Goddess of the dark—sleep, dreams, death, winter, and the earth
The Reaper: God of death

Festivities on the Isle of Skye*

Earth Fire: Salute to new life and the first signs of spring (February 1)
Bealtunn: Spring Equinox
Mid-Summer Fire: Summer Equinox
Harvest Fire: Festival to salute the harvest (Aug 1)
Gateway: Passage from summer to winter (October 31/November 1)
Mid-Winter Fire: Winter Equinox

* Author's note: I have taken 'artistic license' when it comes to the names of the tribes, festivities, and gods and goddesses upon the Isle of Skye. The historical evidence is very scant, making it a challenge for me to get an accurate picture of what the names of the tribes living upon Skye during the 4th century would have been. Likewise I could not find any references to their gods and festivities. The Picts were an enigmatic people, and we only have their ruins and symbols to cast light on how they lived and whom they worshipped. To make my setting as authentic as possible, I have studied the rituals and religions of the Celtic peoples of Scotland, Ireland, and Wales of a similar period and have created a culture I feel could have existed.

The culture, language, and religion of the Picts is one largely shrouded in mystery. Unlike my novels set in 7th Century Anglo-Saxon England, which is a reasonably well-documented period, researching 4th Century Isle of Skye proved to be a challenge. Pictish culture is largely an enigma to us. However, they did leave behind a number of fascinating stone ruins, standing stones, and artifacts, as well as a detailed collection of symbolic art.

I created the four tribes of The Winged Isle from Pictish animal symbols. This is not a far-fetched idea; many Iron and Bronze-age peoples identified themselves with animal symbols. The clans we identify with Scotland did not appear until a few centuries later.

Cast of characters
For those of you who have read THE WARRIOR BROTHERS OF SKYE, understanding who is who in THE PICT WARS shouldn't be too much of a stretch. However, I am aware that my cast of characters is gradually expanding (especially since I've now thrown another tribe into the mix!). So here are all the characters, and their relationships to each other, categorized by tribe:

The Eagle tribe
Galan mac Muin: Eagle chieftain wed to **Tea** with two sons, **Muin** and **Aaron**.
Tarl mac Muin: younger brother of The Eagle chieftain, wed to **Lucrezia** with one daughter, **Fina** (they had three sons who died in childhood: **Bradhg**, **Fionn**, and **Ciaran**)
Donnel mac Muin: youngest brother of The Eagle chieftain, wed to **Eithni** (healer) with one son and two daughters: **Talor** (son from his first marriage), **Bonnie**, and **Eara**
Ailene: the seer at Dun Ringill
Gavina: Muin's former lover

The Boar tribe
Varar mac Urcal: Boar chieftain
Urcal mac Wrad: previous Boar chieftain – the eldest of three sons: **Wurgest** and **Loxa** (all three deceased)
Morag: Varar's sister

The Wolf tribe
Wid mac Manus: Wolf chieftain, wed to **Alana** with two sons, **Calum** and **Bred** (deceased).

Fingal mac Diarmid: Wolf warrior

The Stag tribe
Tadhg mac Fortrenn: Stag chieftain, wed to **Erea** with two daughters, **Moira** and **Ana**

The Cruthini (The Serpent tribe)
Cathal mac Calum: Serpent chieftain
Artair: Cathal's brother
Mor: Cathal's daughter
Murdina: seer
Dunchadh (deceased) and **Tamhas**: Cathal's sons
Tormud mac Alec: Boar warrior, now a member of The Serpent tribe

About the Author

Jayne Castel writes Historical Romance set in Dark Ages Britain and Scotland, and Epic Fantasy Romance. Her vibrant characters, richly researched historical settings, extensive world-building and action-packed adventure romance transport readers back to forgotten times and imaginary worlds.

Jayne is the author of the Amazon bestselling BRIDES OF SKYE series—a Medieval Scottish Romance trilogy about three strong-willed sisters and the men who love them. In love with all things Scottish, she also writes romances set in 4th Century Isle of Skye ... sexy Pict warriors anyone?

When she's not writing, Jayne is reading (and re-reading) her favorite authors, learning French, cooking Italian, and taking her dog, Juno, for walks. She lives in New Zealand's beautiful South Island.

Jayne won the 2017 RWNZ Koru Award (Short, Sexy Category) for her novel, ITALIAN UNDERCOVER AFFAIR.

Get Jayne's FREE prequel short story to THE WARRIOR BROTHERS OF SKYE series: THE FIRST-BORN SON.

http://www.jaynecastel.com/home/sign-up

Connect with Jayne online:
www.jaynecastel.com
www.facebook.com/JayneCastelRomance/
Twitter: @JayneCastel
Email: contact@jaynecastel.com

Made in the USA
Monee, IL
08 March 2021